# "I wish…I wish you would be my mommy for our vacation," River said

"No way, River. I said it had to be something we could do. And having J.J. for a mother…. Pick something else. How about a new doll or a trip to the zoo or a puppy?"

"I have a doll and we go to the zoo all the time." She frowned, interlocking her fingers. "I *do* want a puppy, but I want a mommy more."

"Choose the puppy, honey," Raven advised. "J.J. is not going to be your mother—real, pretend or otherwise. And that's final."

"Please, Daddy," she whispered. "Please let J.J. be my mommy for a little while. I'll be good forever and ever if you say yes."

Raven closed his eyes. "Ah, sweetheart. It's not because you're bad," he assured her softly, cradling her close. "You know that."

"But I want a mommy more than anything in the whole world." Her voice was muffled against the front of his shirt. "Even more than a puppy."

J.J. felt laughter fighting with tears. How could Raven resist such a plea? For that matter, how could she?

**Day Leclaire** and her family live in the midst of a maritime forest on a small island off the coast of North Carolina. Despite the yearly storms that batter them and the frequent power outages, they find the beautiful climate, superb fishing and unbeatable seascape more than adequate compensation. One of their first acquisitions upon moving to Hatteras Island was a cat named Fuzzy. He has recently discovered that laps are wonderful places to curl up and nap—and that Day's son really was kidding when he named the hamster Cat Food.

Day Leclaire has recently been nominated for a *Romantic Times* **Career Achievement Award** in the love and laughter category.

Day Leclaire's next romance **THE NINE-DOLLAR DADDY** will be out in March 1999 as part of our brand-new miniseries *Texas Men Wanted!* Look out for the first *Texas Men Wanted!* book in January from Heather MacAllister!

## Books by Day Leclaire

HARLEQUIN ROMANCE®

3028—JINXED
3139—WHERE THERE'S A WILL
3285—TO CATCH A GHOST
3301—ONCE A COWBOY
3338—WHO'S HOLDING THE BABY?
3361—MAIL-ORDER BRIDEGROOM
3376—ONE-NIGHT WIFE
3404—MAKE BELIEVE ENGAGEMENT

3433—TEMPORARY HUSBAND*~
3438—ACCIDENTAL WIFE*~
3440—SHOTGUN MARRIAGE*
3457—THE SECRET BABY
3486—HER SECRET SANTA~
3495—THE TWENTY-FOUR-HOUR BRIDE
3508—THE BOSS, THE BABY AND
     THE BRIDE

*Fairytale Wedding trilogy
~Shortlisted for *Romantic Times* **Reviewers Choice Award**
for best Harlequin Romance.

Don't miss any of our special offers. Write to us at the following address for information on our newest releases.

Harlequin Reader Service
U.S.: 3010 Walden Ave., P.O. Box 1325, Buffalo, NY 14269
Canadian: P.O. Box 609, Fort Erie, Ont. L2A 5X3

# Day Leclaire

## The Miracle Wife

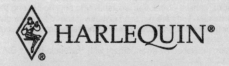

HARLEQUIN®

TORONTO • NEW YORK • LONDON
AMSTERDAM • PARIS • SYDNEY • HAMBURG
STOCKHOLM • ATHENS • TOKYO • MILAN • MADRID
PRAGUE • WARSAW • BUDAPEST • AUCKLAND

To Luann Smith,
with much love, for all her help and support.

ISBN 0-373-03523-3

THE MIRACLE WIFE

First North American Publication 1998.

Copyright © 1998 by Day Totton Smith.

**Printed in U.S.A.**

# PROLOGUE

Once upon a time there lived a fairy named Justice. On one thing all fairies agreed... Justice was the most beautiful of their people. Her skin rivaled the color of fresh moonlit snow, her hair gleamed blacker than a dragon's hide. And her eyes appeared as dark as a moonless night, yet glittered with a fiery passion. But it was her inner beauty, the life-light that shone brighter than a thousand suns that made people love her the most.

Page 1, *The Great Dragon Hunt*
by Jack Rabbitt

RIVER SIERRA studied the birthday cake her housekeeper had placed on the table. The flame from six pink candles danced gleefully—five for each birthday plus one to grow on. She wished her daddy could have stayed while she blew them out. But maybe if he had, he'd have asked what her wish was and...

And everyone knew that wishes didn't come true if you told.

She planted her elbows on the table and cupped her chin in her palms. This was a very important wish. The most important she'd ever made. She gnawed nervously at her lower lip. It was also a wish her daddy wouldn't like very much. He might even get mad if he knew she'd made it. She considered the possibility with a frown.

Weren't wishes secret? If she didn't tell anyone, wouldn't the wish stay hidden even from grown-ups? Maybe her father wouldn't find out about this one since it was magic. River worried her lip some more. It might work, *if* she didn't tell. It would be hard. Very hard. She'd never kept a secret from her daddy before, but this time—

River tilted her head to one side, watching as a fat drop of wax threatened to splatter on the perfect white icing. Okay. She'd keep her wish a secret from everyone. Well... Everyone, except Gem. And she didn't count since she was magic, too. Of course, Daddy had said Gem was a computer, which made her just a machine. But that *had* to be wrong. Gem was real.

"WISH IS NECESSARY TO SUCCESSFULLY EXTINGUISH FLAMES," the computer announced.

"You mean it won't work if I don't wish before I blow out the candles?"

"AFFIRMATIVE."

She eyed her father's present—another Jack Rabbitt storybook filled with the most beautiful pictures she'd ever seen. He'd even bought one of the paintings from the book and hung it on her bedroom wall. She loved the painting, loved it with all the passion her newly five-year-old body could summon. It was about a fairy riding a butterfly, a fairy with long black hair—hair just like River's very own. In the book, the fairy could grant wishes. But whether that included birthday wishes, River wasn't sure.

"HAS WISH BEEN MADE?" Gem inquired.

"No."

"DANGER OF FIRE HAZARD IMMINENT."

"What?"

"HURRY."

"Oh. Okay. I'm hurrying." This was it. If she got in trouble with Daddy for making the wish, she'd sit on her bed and read her books and look at her painting. That wouldn't be so bad. Not if the wish came true. River squeezed her eyes shut and then whispered, "I want a mommy for my very own. And I want her to be just like the fairy in my painting." With that, she opened her eyes and blew out the candles.

It was done. She'd made her wish. Now, she just had to wait for it to come true. Because Gem had told her...

Birthday wishes always came true.

J.J. Randell entered her office at Blackstone's, a firm that specialized in "procuring" items of value for their clients. Whether the item held emotional value or monetary, didn't matter. Whatever you wanted, Blackstone's could get it. It had been her workplace for almost a year, thanks to a touch of nepotism on behalf of her brother-in-law, Mathias Blackstone. In the months she'd been employed here, she'd found it a highly satisfying occupation. Certainly better than her previous one.

"What's Mr. Blackstone's schedule today?" J.J. questioned Gem, the new computer system they'd recently installed. It surprised her that Mathias hadn't arrived at work, yet—a first in her experience.

"MR. BLACKSTONE UNAVAILABLE. PLEASE ACCESS MEMO WAITING ON DESKTOP COMPUTER AND FOLLOW INSTRUCTIONS IMMEDIATELY."

The distinctly feminine voice issued from nearby speakers, its humanlike quality still enough of an oddity to amaze J.J. An interactive computer. Incredible. It was almost like being on *Star Trek.* "Okay, no problem."

She turned on the desktop machine and called up the memo, scanning it in delight. "I don't believe it," she murmured. *Finally!* Mathias was finally offering her the opportunity she'd dreamed of since joining the firm—to assist him in granting a Christmas wish.

It was one of Mathias's pet projects, a generous extension of his bill-paying line of work. For the month of December he became a "Secret Santa," working behind the scenes for those in need and anonymously fulfilling their dearest wishes. Apparently he now trusted her enough to take over one of his Santa projects. Though considering this was only October, he must have decided she could use a running start.

She frowned as she absorbed the scant details. A five-year-old girl named River Sierra from Denver, Colorado, was to be granted her dearest desire. A seat on the next plane awaited J.J. at Sea-Tac Airport. She was to leave without delay and to keep the project absolutely confidential. No one, other than herself and Mathias, could be privy to her plan. How odd.

"Gem, do you have any further information on River Sierra?"

"ERROR NUMBER FIVE-OH-NINE. UNAUTHORIZED ACCESS REQUESTED."

"That doesn't make any sense," J.J. argued. "Why don't I have access? I've been told to grant this kid's request. How am I supposed to do that without all the necessary background information?"

There was a momentary silence, then the computer came on-line again. "INFORMATION UNAVAILABLE," the machine repeated stubbornly. "PLEASE PROCEED TO AIRPORT. ONE HOUR FIFTY-NINE MINUTES REMAIN UNTIL DEPARTURE."

She stared blankly for an instant. "That can't be right. Gem, you must have made a mistake. I can't get everything done. I have to finish up the project Mathias requested by noon, before going home to pack. Not to mention the calls I'm supposed to—"

"NEGATIVE. ACTIVITIES WILL NOT FIT IN CURRENT TIME FRAME."

She shook her head in bewilderment. "But... I don't understand. What's the rush?"

"INFORMATION UNAVAILABLE. PLEASE—"

"I know. I know," she interrupted with a sigh. "Please proceed to airport. One hour fifty-nine minutes remain until departure."

"CORRECTION. ONE HOUR FIFTY-EIGHT MINUTES REMAIN."

J.J. grimaced. She'd learned that arguing with the computer was utterly pointless. She never won. "Do you at least know how long I'll be in Colorado? What am I supposed to do about clothes?"

"INFORMATION—"

"—not available. Just great."

This didn't make any sense. Why the sudden hurry? Surely a few hours' delay wouldn't make that much difference. Unless... Her eyes narrowed. Unless this was some sort of test. Perhaps Mathias wanted to see how quickly she responded and how flexible an attitude she had. That might explain it. After all, what other reason could there be for such unreasonable speed?

Well, fine. Her boss required fast and easy? She could do that. Sure she could. Heck, she'd learned at her father's knee that you didn't question the boss. Not unless you wanted your head taken off. Her mouth curved into a wry smile. Of course, when she'd learned that handy little lesson, her father *was* her boss. He'd taught her the importance of instant obedience and unquestioning loyalty.

Though her brother-in-law was a far different employer than her father, she owed Mathias. He'd taken her away from her former, soul-eating job and offered an opportunity that few men would have. Determination filled her. He wouldn't find reason to fault her job performance after all he'd done. Whatever he asked, she'd accomplish to the best of her ability.

Opening her soft-sided briefcase, she checked to make sure she had all the connections for her portable computer and the paperwork on the other non-Christmas related projects Mathias had dumped on her desk only yesterday. Odd that this assignment had suddenly received precedence over the other, equally urgent jobs she'd been given. With a shrug, she shoved a handful of files into her briefcase—just in case she ran out of work while in Colorado—and gave her office a quick, assessing glance to see if there was anything else she'd need for the trip. Her gaze fell on the latest Jack Rabbitt book her sister, Jacq, had dropped off just yesterday.

Apparently being the author and illustrator of the most popular line of children's books came with some perks. The picture book was hot off the presses, not even available in stores, and starred a brand-new character—a dragon. That Mathias had been the unwitting model for the fierce, black creature added to its appeal. Jacq certainly had managed to capture some of his more distinct physical attributes. Anyone who knew Mathias would instantly recognize him in the face and posture of this proud, mythic beast.

J.J. picked up the book and ran a hand over the richly embossed cover. Since her assignment involved a little girl, perhaps this would make a good ice-breaker. At any rate, it couldn't hurt. Slipping the book into her briefcase, she zipped the leather case closed.

Just one final chore before she left, J.J. decided, lifting

the phone receiver. A quick call to Jacq to tell her about the trip and then—

"WARNING. ONE HOUR FIFTY-FIVE MINUTES REMAINING. SPEED IS HIGHLY RECOMMENDED."

J.J. hesitated, then hung up the phone with a frustrated sigh. "Okay, okay. I'm going." She could always call Jacq later.

Grabbing her briefcase and coat, she left her office and crossed to the elevators. Despite being rushed, she couldn't help but grin. She'd been given a chance to play Santa. Her very first Christmas wish. How lucky could she get? The elevator arrived and she stepped into the car. Just as the doors snicked closed again she caught a glimpse of a man striding past. She could have sworn it was Mathias. And yet Gem had said—

J.J. shook her head. Nah. It must have been someone who looked like her brother-in-law. After all...

Computers didn't lie.

# CHAPTER ONE

Justice hid behind a clump of ferns and watched the prince, just as she always watched whenever he came to the forest. The first time she'd seen him, she'd fallen in love. She'd never realized fairies were capable of such an emotion. But, apparently, she was different than most, for she loved the prince with all her heart and soul—even more than fairy life itself. Sometimes when he explored the woods, she crept very, very close. So close she could almost reach out and touch him—at least, she could if she weren't so afraid. But fear had always kept her from speaking. Until today. Today, she planned to finally reveal herself and see if maybe…just maybe, he could love her, too.

Page 3, *The Great Dragon Hunt*
by Jack Rabbitt

IT HAD to be the most infuriating moment he'd ever experienced.

Raven Sierra glared balefully at the mob of Denver's less-reputable reporters. Dammit all! They'd enclosed him in an inescapable ring, trapping him in the lobby of his own office building, holding him at bay as if he were a cougar run down by a pack of rabid dogs. If he'd been alone, he'd have fought back, raking them with cutting words and subtle threats, sending them scrambling for cover. But the SOBs had caught him at his most vulnerable.

His five-year-old daughter, River, clung to his leg with one arm while anxiously clutching a rag doll with the other. Every once in a while she'd lift her gaze to his, her glorious silver-blue eyes filled with the certainty that her daddy would rescue them from the noisy onslaught. Soft black bangs feathered her brow and a wash of silken-fine hair shot in a straight curtain to the middle of her back. In silent communion, he slipped his hand through her hair, his long fingers cupping her rounded cheek. Reassured, she relaxed imperceptibly and leaned into his thigh, far too patient and quiet and accepting of Fate's perversity for a child her age. His rage built, communicating itself to well-toned muscles, while a fight-or-flee adrenaline surge threatened to overwhelm his need for calm control.

"Mr. Sierra! We have it on good authority that your days as Denver's most eligible bachelor are about to end. Who's the lucky woman?"

"On good authority?" Raven questioned sharply. "And whose authority would that be?"

"The announcement came from someone within your own organization. We were e-mailed the information."

Raven's eyes narrowed. That explained their presence. But, who within his company would have the nerve to e-mail the press such a blatant lie and risk incurring his wrath? He intended to find out, and whoever it was would be out the door bruised, if not wiser. He glanced over his shoulders toward the bank of elevators. Where the *hell* was security? They should have arrived long ago to clear off this pack of yapping dogs. Until they made an appearance, he'd have to wait—not his usual method of handling a situation such as this.

"Come on, Mr. Untouchable," another reporter urged. "This is too good to ignore. Someone's obviously managed to put a collar around your neck. Spill it. Who's holding the leash?"

The coarse laughter that followed had Raven clenching his hands. How he'd love to cut loose with these animals. Unfortunately, with River at his side, he didn't dare. He remained silent, though he made certain his gaze promised retribution.

"When's the wedding?" demanded another reporter.

"Is she pregnant?" A cynical-eyed blonde threw the question at him—Ms. Lark, the most aggressive of the bunch. "Is that why you two are getting married?"

"Who is she? You know we're gonna find out eventually, so you might as well tell us."

As though the reporters' questions summoned her, a woman stepped through the doors of Sierra Consortium. She paused, caught in a shaft of sunlight that poured through the glass wall of the lobby. Most women he knew would have been disconcerted by the sudden spotlight. Not this one. She went perfectly still as she took stock of her surroundings. It reminded him of a lone doe entering a meadow, testing the winds for the scent of danger. Wary, rather than shy. Determined, but not foolish about it.

The woman was also gorgeous, Raven acknowledged reluctantly—tall, slender and devastatingly elegant. Her clothes were impeccable, as was her hair and makeup. She carried herself with the assurance of someone not easily disconcerted. Obviously she'd been around. He'd have expected a woman like that to have a brittle so-

phistication that penetrated clear to her soul, like the
blond reporter snarling at his heels.

But even as he tried to pin the accusation on this
woman, he knew he was mistaken. Rather, he sensed a
softness, a radiant sweetness his grandmother used to
call a "gold spirit." "Those are the ones you marry,"
Nawna had told him the week before she'd died.
"They're pure on the inside, where it counts. You wait.
Wait until you find a pure one. Then you cling to her
and never let go. She will close the circle. She will heal
and complete you." He shook off the memory, furious
with himself for giving credence to an old woman's foolish fantasies. For that's all they were. And with one re-
grettable exception, he'd weeded each and every fantasy
from his life—and from his daughter's.

Spying the reception desk, the woman deserted her
position in the sunlight and crossed the lobby. Raven
watched, swearing beneath his breath. She moved with
a supple, rhythmic stride that attracted instant attention.
Of course. Beauty *and* grace. He'd always found it a
deadly combination. Consciously or not, women like this
drew men. Even if the trap of physical appeal could be
avoided, they captured the unwary with every sway of
hip and sweep of hand, their silent music more potent
than a siren's lure. As hardened as he'd become, he
could still hear the call, sense the subtle pull.

She was forbidden desire.

Pausing at the desk, she questioned the man on duty,
listening carefully to his response. Before she even
turned, he sensed it, a gut instinct warning that she'd
come for him. His mouth twisted. Another of Nawna's
"gifts," one he hadn't quite eradicated. Sure enough,
her head swiveled in his direction and hair as long and
richly black as his daughter's drifted in a slow, dark slide
across one shoulder. Their gazes locked, honey brown
clashing with raven black. To his surprise, she didn't

approach. Instead the woman slowly circled the press of reporters until she stood behind them. Setting her briefcase at her feet, she folded her arms across her chest and propped one shoulder against a nearby pillar.

And then she smiled.

He paid a huge price for that one smile. The focus he'd divided between the woman and the reporters slipped for a costly split second, arrowing in on her with unmistakable intensity. The reporters didn't miss a beat. Almost as one, they turned. The crowd shifted ever so slightly, providing a clear view of the woman.

At his side, he heard River catch her breath. "Daddy! It's her, it's her! She's come to give me my wish. Hurry or she'll fly away."

Before he could stop his impetuous daughter, she ripped free of his hold and plunged into the tightly packed crowd. With an agility borne of desperation, she wriggled through the forest of legs, intent on achieving her goal. Releasing a string of pent-up curses, Raven started after her. She disappeared from view for a horrifying moment. Then he saw her skid to a halt in front of the woman. The two were completely encircled by the crowd of reporters—with Raven on the outside of that magical ring.

"You came!" he heard River exclaim as she flung herself at the woman. Even more startling, the woman acted as though she knew his daughter, laughing at the child's enthusiasm and scooping her into a warm embrace. He could hear River's piping voice, hear that she asked a question, but couldn't make out the exact words.

Only two more reporters separated him from his daughter. Raven didn't bother with niceties. Dropping a heavy hand on their shoulders, he shoved them from his path. The woman's attention was still focused on the girl she held, foolishly unaware of the trouble she'd summoned by touching his child. She hesitated, taking a moment to consider her response to River's question. What the *hell* was going on? Then she nodded. With a shriek of delight, River wrapped her arms around the woman's neck.

Raven planted himself in front of the two, fighting to keep his voice low, struggling to subdue the deadly tone. He didn't succeed. "Take your hands off my kid."

River swiveled to face him, her expression lit with the purest joy he'd ever seen. "Daddy! She said yes. Justice is going to be my new mommy."

A blinding series of flashbulbs exploded around J.J. and she blinked in confusion. Surely she couldn't have heard correctly. What had River said? "Wait just a minute! I didn't—" Her words were drowned beneath an avalanche of shouted questions and the sudden press of the surrounding reporters jockeying for a better position.

"What's your name, lady?"

"When's the wedding?"

"Where'd you two meet?"

"How did you convince Mr. Untouchable to pop the big question?"

"When's your baby due?"

J.J. had faced the press countless times before. But never like this, never when they were in a feeding frenzy. Desperate for an avenue of escape her gaze lifted to the man planted directly in front of her. She'd been told at the reception desk that he was Raven Sierra, River's father. The name fit.

He was as dark and sharp-eyed as a raven, with a countenance as cold and craggy as the Sierra peaks. His eyes reminded her of pitch…black and unrelenting and all-consuming. And he disturbed her in ways she preferred to keep safely untouched. There was something about him… Some indefinable quality that slipped past her guard and breached the defenses she'd spent years erecting.

Her eyes narrowed. It wasn't his appearance that attracted her. She wouldn't consider him conventionally handsome. Sure, he had great features—high, flaring cheekbones, a no-nonsense, squared chin and a broad, well-defined mouth. But his nose had taken a beating or two and his eyes were far too intense, filled with the light of raw passion, betraying him as a man who had walked the wild side on more than one occasion. His hair emphasized that dark streak. He wore it long, the thick waves stubbornly untamed.

And then it struck her, enabling her to recognize the underlying appeal. He'd been through the same wars she had. Fought the same battles. Received the same scars. Whether he knew it or not, they were kindred spirits. They were connected on a level few would understand. That's why he'd been able to penetrate her defenses with a single look. He knew where to find the hidden passageways.

Unfortunately she'd done something that had stirred the warrior in him—something connected to his daughter. That made him twice as dangerous. Instead of working in concert together, she'd managed to pit them one against the other. She closed her eyes, summoning the energy the coming confrontation would entail. Whatever she'd done, she'd better be able to rectify the situation or she'd pay dearly. This was a man who didn't lose.

Taking a deep breath, she looked at him. He didn't say a word. He didn't have to. She could feel the rage building behind his rigid expression, knew he'd be only too happy to toss her to the scavenging reporters scrambling behind him. What in the world had just happened? How had she gone from innocent bystander to center ring in this media circus? She gave reconciliation a final ditch effort.

"Please," she whispered, clutching River close.

She truly thought he'd ignore her entreaty. Winter had

descended on this particular mountaintop, leaving it in frigid isolation. He plucked his daughter from her arms and tossed the little girl over his shoulder. And then, just as she expected to be deserted, he wrapped a heavy arm around her. Shock vied with relief. It would seem she'd found herself a noble warrior after all, one who'd conduct their battle in private. Tucking her close, he forged a path through the opposition. At the last possible instant she remembered to snatch up her briefcase. Thank goodness she hadn't forgotten that.

He hustled them toward the far end of the lobby, reporters dogging their heels and shouting questions. The instant they reached a bank of elevators, the doors parted and a half-dozen security men tumbled from the car.

"Sorry, boss," one of them gasped. "The damn thing shut off on us halfway down. Your computer kept telling us we'd made some sort of error."

"Get rid of our visitors," Raven ordered.

"No problem. We'll get right on it."

Still maintaining a protective stance, Raven shepherded them into the car. "My office," he instructed as the doors closed, leaving their pursuers at the mercy of the security men.

To J.J.'s amazement, Gem responded to the request. "AFFIRMATIVE, MR. SIERRA. WILL REACH DESTINATION IN ONE MINUTE, FORTY-FIVE POINT SEVEN SECONDS."

"Gem, what are you doing here?" J.J. questioned in surprise.

"IDENTIFY PLEASE."

"It's me. J.J. Randell."

"ONE MOMENT. ACCESSING." A series of high-pitched beeps emitted from the speakers. Then Gem came on-line again. "WELCOME TO SIERRA CONSORTIUM, MS. RANDELL. HOW WAS YOUR TRIP?"

"Can it, Gem." Raven cut in. "This isn't the time for pointless chitchat, especially coming from a computer."

"ERROR FOUR-NINETEEN. REQUEST UN-CLEAR. PLEASE REPHRASE."

"Shut up," he growled. "Is that clear enough?"

"AFFIRMATIVE, MR. SIERRA. SHUTTING UP."

He turned his attention to J.J. and she braced herself for the first wave of his attack. "Okay, sweetheart. Your turn. What the hell are you doing here? And how do you know about Gem? Are you associated with SSI?"

"SSI?" she repeated in confusion.

"Security Systems, International. Nick Colter's company. They invented the computer."

"Oh. No, I'm not. We just bought the system recently, ourselves. I guess they use the same voice for all their programs."

Apparently satisfied with her response, he nodded dismissively. "Fascinating. Now, once again. Who the hell are you and what are you doing here?"

"I'm J.J. Randell and I work for Blackstone's. It's a procurement firm out of Seattle owned by Mathias—"

"Blackstone! Son of a—" He broke off, shooting a wary glance at his all-too-attentive daughter. "He set this up, didn't he?" he demanded in an undertone.

Her confusion grew. "Set what up?"

"You. He arranged for you to be here."

Somehow she suspected she'd regret confirming his guess. Still… She had a job to accomplish—a job that grew more complicated by the minute. "Yes, he sent me."

Raven shifted closer. It was a tiny movement, no more than changing his balance from one foot to the other. And yet, the spacious car shrank, becoming far too small to contain her, one small girl and the infuriated male at her side. He seemed to loom above her, his gaze gathering her up and holding her with frightening intensity.

"Well, you can hightail it back to Seattle and tell your boss my answer hasn't changed."

J.J. stared, stunned. She'd been here all of fifteen minutes and she'd already blown her very first Christmas wish? "You want me to leave?"

Instantly River burst into tears. She grabbed at her father's belt and tugged frantically. "Daddy, no! Don't send her away. She came to give me my wish. You can't let her leave."

The change in him was instantaneous. The fury eased from his expression, concern seeping into his eyes and voice. "What wish, honey? What are you talking about."

River clutched her rag doll even closer and flashed a quick guilty look from her father to J.J. "My birthday wish. I made a wish and Justice is here to make it come true. She said so."

"Who's Justice?"

River pointed at J.J. "That's Justice. Don't you 'member? She's the fairy in my book. I wished for her and she came."

J.J. swallowed. Uh-oh. Matters had just taken a serious turn for the worse. She addressed River. "I'm not a fairy, sweetheart. I'm a real person."

The little girl appeared far from convinced, but before she could argue, the doors parted and J.J. hastened from the car into a large, empty reception area, relieved to have the extra maneuvering room. She forced herself to turn and confront Raven. "Look… It's obvious that there's been some sort of misunderstanding. Perhaps we could all sit down and sort it out."

"Sure." Raven lowered his daughter to the floor. "We'll start working it out right away so you can catch the next plane home." He realized his mistake the instant River teared up again. He pointed to a tall door, composed of curved sections of mixed-wood inlay. Each piece fit into the next in an intriguing pattern of light and dark. It took an instant for her to see the raven hidden in the pattern. ''Wait for me in my office.''

Without a word, she pushed open the door, leaving father and daughter to talk in private. His office reminded her somewhat of her brother-in-law's. Like Mathias, Raven preferred an absence of colors. But rather than the study in black and white that had once dominated Blackstone's, wood complemented the strong white walls and dove gray Berber carpet. It gave a warmth to the room that took her by surprise. She'd expected something cold and sterile. Instead the decor offered unexpected insights into Sierra's nature.

The surface of his desk duplicated the door to his office, the intricately carved wood protected by a heavy sheet of glass. It was a beautiful piece of workmanship. As she studied it, she noticed something she'd missed before. The raven hidden in the pattern flew over a rippling stream, its wings spread wide as though to embrace the expanse of water. Did it symbolize his daughter, River? It seemed likely. For such a hard man, it revealed a vulnerability she found disconcerting.

Opposite the desk she noted a small sitting area, the tables made of the same inlaid wood as Raven's desk and office door. But it was the corner of the room nearest his desk that drew her, an area clearly designed for River's exclusive use. A miniature desk and bookcase took up most of the space. Behind the desk, childish crayon drawings completely covered the stark white wall. Clearly the man had a soft spot for his daughter, if he allowed her to color on his office walls. Scattered in between the colorful drawings they'd hung photos and pictures cut from various magazines.

J.J. crossed the room to take a closer look. Centered among all the drawings and framed by brightly colored scribbles she found an article about Jack Rabbitt, along with a photo of one of her sister's storybook illustrations. The article was almost a year old, and one J.J. remembered well.

The caption beneath the photo read, "Jack Rabbitt—the author and illustrator whose identity remains shrouded in secrecy—now ranks number one with children worldwide." Of course, Jacq had revealed her identity not long after that article had been released and sold the painting they'd highlighted in order to raise money for a child's bone marrow operation.

J.J. caught her lip between her teeth. Even after a full year, the featured painting still had the power to disconcert her. For some reason, it was one of her sister's favorites. It portrayed the fairy, Justice, riding a butterfly. The wings of the butterfly swept upward, concealing the naked fairy from the shoulders down, while sunlight turned the wings to gossamer, detailing the fairy's silhouette through a swirl of soft color. Of course, the identity of the fairy was unmistakable.

It was J.J.

Just as Jacq had used her future husband as a model for the dragon, Nemesis, she'd used her sister as a then-unknowing model for the fairy. When confronted, Jacq had explained the symbolism. She'd hoped J.J. would one day break free and learn to fly, like the fairy in her storybooks. Well, J.J. had done her best. Her first wobbly step toward that freedom had come the day she'd left her father's PR firm to work at Blackstone's. And now she'd embarked on another formative step—fulfilling her first Christmas wish.

Unfortunately she currently found herself in the uncomfortable position of having to explain to a five-year-old child that she wasn't really a magical fairy. Just great. She'd simply tell River, "I'm no fairy, sweetheart. I've simply come to give you a wish." The poor kid would understand the distinction, right? Sure she would.

J.J. shook her head in disgust. What the heck was she supposed to do now?

As though in response to her silent question, the office door opened and Raven Sierra stepped across the threshold. "My secretary is watching River while we talk," he said, sealing the door behind him. "We have a problem."

"I suspected as much."

"My daughter is of the opinion that you're a fairy who came here to grant her wish. She insists that's what you told her. Would you mind explaining why you'd do something so reprehensible?"

J.J.'s eyes widened in alarm. "There's been a misunderstanding."

His jaw clenched, but he kept his voice as civil as hers. "Yes, there has." A humorless smile slashed across his face. "And you made it."

It would seem the battle was well and truly engaged. Fine. She'd been in more conflicts than she could count. What was another one? She lifted her chin and held her ground. "I did come to grant River her wish, but I never claimed to be a fairy. I think she's confusing me with the one in the Jack Rabbitt books." Suddenly remembering the gift she'd brought, she snapped her fingers and glanced around for her briefcase. "Hang on a sec. I have something that might help."

"What do you mean you've come to grant her wish?"

Spying her briefcase resting against the leg of his desk, J.J. stooped beside it. "I thought you said you knew about Mathias and the wishes."

Perhaps if she'd been looking at him she'd have had some warning. Instead the heavy hand that clamped on her arm and drew her to her feet came as a complete— and unnerving—surprise. "Mathias sent you to give *my* daughter a wish?"

If only he weren't holding her so close. She drew a

shaky breath, but that only made it worse. Now she had his scent to contend with in addition to the powerful play of muscles across his chest and along his arms. "He— he does that. Surprises people with Christmas wishes." Her eyes widened as she belatedly recalled the directive to keep the project absolutely confidential. Dammit all. This was Raven's fault! If he hadn't been touching her, she wouldn't have lost her concentration and revealed so much.

"A Christmas wish," he repeated. "In case you hadn't noticed, it's not Christmas."

"I guess he decided to give me a head start." It sounded lame, even to her ears.

"I don't need Blackstone giving my child anything— especially not wishes."

Perhaps she should start over. She'd made a number of assumptions that under other circumstances, she'd never have done. Apparently, since leaving her father's PR firm, she'd lost her edge. Carefully she eased from his hold. It helped. A little. "Look, I'm new at granting wishes," she confessed. "To be honest, your daughter is my first assignment. So, perhaps I'm not going about it exactly right."

"Have you any idea what her wish is?"

His question resurrected that horrible moment downstairs, when they were besieged by reporters and River had said... Said... "Justice is going to be my new mommy!"

J.J. moistened her lips. "Please tell me it isn't what she mentioned downstairs. She wants a...a *mother?*"

His eyes caught fire again and she realized she'd run full tilt into a father's protective instinct—an instinct that had unquestioningly slipped into overdrive. "You told her that's why you came," he accused. "My daughter is sitting in the other room indulging unrealistic fantasies about weddings and mothers and fairy-tale endings. And you're responsible.''

''I came to grant her a wish. That much is true.''

''What wish were you instructed to grant?''

Heaven help her. If he was angry before, he was going to be furious when he heard her answer. ''I don't know,'' she whispered.

''You don't know?''

How could three tiny words sound so deadly? ''The memo just gave her name and instructed me to come here and grant her wish,'' J.J. hastened to explain.

''Let me see this memo.''

''I don't have it. It was on my computer at work.'' Inspiration struck. ''Ask Gem. She was there.''

His eyebrows winged upward. ''My computer system is privy to the memos at Blackstone?''

''Oh, right. I guess they wouldn't be interconnected, would they?''

''They better not be.''

And yet…Gem had recognized her in the elevator. J.J. fought an overwhelming sense of bewilderment. She needed to think, to puzzle the problem through—assuming Raven gave her a chance to do that. ''Look, I don't understand any of this. Mathias grants wishes that are really straightforward. And good-hearted. He'd never deliberately—''

''Do *not* sing Mathias Blackstone's praises to me,'' Raven cut her off with unmistakable fury. ''I know all I need to about your boss. He's a procurer.'' He made it sound tainted. ''He'll pay any price or go to any extreme to obtain whatever treasure he's after at the moment. Even if it involves hurting a little girl.''

''No! That's not true. He's a Secret Santa.'' Oh, no! She'd done it again. What was it about Raven? How did he manage to pull words from her mouth that had no business being there? ''Mathias gives people wishes free of charge,'' she explained with a sigh. ''He's the most generous man I know.''

''My daughter is desperate for a mother. Not any mother, but a mother who happens to be a fairy. A fairy who looks just like you. How's he going to grant her wish?''

He had her with that one. ''I suppose he sent me because I *do* look like Justice. I guess I'm in the best position to handle the problem.''

''You both could have handled the problem by not showing up,'' he growled. ''Before it was a child's fantasy. A dream. Now she thinks that dream can become reality. Well, thanks, but no thanks.'' Swearing beneath his breath, he swung away from her. ''How did Mathias know about her wish?''

''I assume someone told him.''

Raven turned to face her again, his eyes brimming with suspicion. ''Who?''

''I haven't a clue, though Mathias has incredible sources.''

''He'd have to. *I* didn't even know about River's wish until five minutes ago.''

''Someone had to,'' she insisted gently. ''Even if you didn't.''

''And Mathias discovered my daughter wanted you for a mother and, without any warning, pitched you into the middle of it.'' His sarcasm cut deep. ''How kind of him.''

He'd touched on a sore point. She didn't appreciate being manipulated, and right at this moment, she definitely felt as though she'd been used. It was all too reminiscent of the years she'd spent working for her father—long, painful, soul-corrupting years. J.J. lowered her head, fighting the cynical side of her nature. There had to be some other explanation for Mathias's actions. He knew her history and wouldn't hurt her that way. Her hands collapsed into tight fists. *Please don't let him have set her up like this.*

"Perhaps he didn't realize that was her wish," she suggested, fighting a creeping despair. "Perhaps he just knew she had one and—"

Raven cut her off. "Don't bother covering for him. Face it. He's using you and my daughter to get at me. How noble."

That caught her attention. Mathias hoped to get at Raven? "What does he want from you?"

"He didn't even tell you that much?"

She shook her head. "Nor do I believe he'd use a child to obtain a procurement any more than he'd use me. Mathias isn't like that." Although he *had* used Jacq to fulfill a wish one time. But that had been different. Still... Doubts assailed her yet again.

"Let's just say that your precious boss has been in touch for the past six months in an effort to purchase some property of mine. I've refused him every single time, but the man doesn't give up."

"He is rather determined," J.J. conceded.

"So now he's using a more ruthless method. My daughter. He's trying to force my compliance through her." He approached, his eyes reflecting a harsh warning. "It's a mistake he's going to regret."

Somehow she suspected her brother-in-law wasn't the only one who would experience regrets. She struggled for composure. "Mathias wouldn't do anything to harm your daughter. Nor would I. Tell me how you want to handle the situation with River and I'll do it. Will that satisfy you?"

"It's a start."

"So? What do you suggest?"

"First, you're going to convince my daughter that you're not a fairy. Then you're going to explain that you can't fulfill her wish. Understood?"

"Yes."

He crowded close again, the warmth of his body invading hers. Did the man have no sense of personal space? Apparently not. "I'm warning you, Ms. Randell. Be very careful what you say. In case you hadn't noticed, I'm extremely protective of my daughter."

A thousand sarcastic retorts leapt to her tongue and she successfully bit back every last one of them. Years of practice helped. When she fixed her gaze on him, she knew it would be empty of all expression. "I understand," she replied evenly. "I wouldn't want to do anything to hurt her."

He studied her for a moment longer, no doubt assessing her sincerity. Finally he nodded. "I'll bring her in."

"Will you allow me to speak to her privately?"

It went against his better judgment, she could tell. Tension radiated from him, his muscles clenching as if he were a predator on the verge of attack. "Don't screw this up, Ms. Randell."

"I'll do my best not to."

"You better hope your best is good enough."

He left the room and J.J. took a deep breath. Then another. Dear heaven, what had Mathias been thinking? Had he completely lost his mind? She wished she had enough time to call and demand an explanation, but somehow she doubted that was a possibility. Fighting for control, she stooped beside her briefcase again and removed the Jack Rabbitt book she'd brought for River. Thank goodness she'd tossed it in.

She suspected it just might change everything.

# CHAPTER TWO

Fausta was the oldest and wisest fairy in the entire kingdom. And she knew more magic than all the fairies put together. Rumor had it, she even knew how to tame the great dragon, Nemesis—or at least how to win a favor from the dark beast. It was this ability Justice wanted to learn more than anything else in the whole world.

She and the prince had continued to meet in secret. But that secret wouldn't last much longer. Soon they would be forced to part unless... Unless Justice coaxed a favor from Nemesis.

Page 10, *The Great Dragon Hunt*
Jack Rabbitt

THE door swung open and River peeked around, cradling her rag doll to her shoulder. She appeared absurdly tiny in comparison to the massive wood panel. ''Justice?'' she whispered. ''Are you there?''

J.J. stepped from the shadows so she could be seen. "I'm right here, sweetheart."

With a broad grin, the little girl erupted into the room. "I was afraid you turned back into a fairy and flew away." She threw herself against J.J., her arms desperately tight, as though she truly were worried that her "fairy" might disappear at any second.

J.J. released her breath in a frustrated sigh. Time to set the poor thing straight. Destroying River's illusions would be one of the most difficult tasks she'd ever faced. But what choice did she have? This whole "wish" business had gotten seriously out of hand. "I didn't change back into a fairy because I'm not a fairy," she explained gently. "I'm a real person, just like you."

River shrugged, clearly unconcerned. "I know. Fairies can do that for a little while."

J.J.'s brows pulled together. "They can?"

The little girl giggled. "Didn't you know that? Is that why you don't think you're a fairy? Did you forget when you turned into a lady?"

"No. I—" Good grief. This wasn't getting her anywhere. Here, she'd been in a flat-out panic about causing permanent psychological damage to the poor kid. It had never occurred to her that River wouldn't believe what she had to say. Determinedly, she held out the Jack Rabbitt book, *The Great Dragon Hunt*. "I brought this for you as a present. It's brand-new."

River's face lit up. "Oh, thank you!" She stared at the cover with a touch of awe. "A dragon. I didn't know there were dragons, too."

Oh, great. "Not real dragons, honey. Look. Let me show you something inside." Turning to the back flap, she pointed to the picture of Jacq. "That's Jack Rabbitt. Her name's pretend just like her stories. She's my sister. Her real name's Jacqueline Blackstone. She's the one who writes the books and draws the pictures. She makes them up. Understand? They're all make-believe, not real.''

"Is she a fairy, too?"

J.J. groaned. Clearly she was having limited success explaining reality to the little girl. It would seem the stubbornness gene had made a successful pass from father to daughter. "No. She's a real person, just like me. She invented the dragons and fairies and used people as models for her drawings. That's why I look like Justice. But my real name is J.J.''

"Where do you keep your wings when you're bein' a person?'' River circled J.J., tilting her head from side to side. "Do they come off? Do you hang them up in your closet? Or are they invisible?''

J.J. twisted around to face the little girl. "Sweetheart, please listen to me. I don't have wings. I'm not a fairy. Fairies are pretend. Do you understand pretend?''

River simply nodded, not in the least troubled by the revelation. "That's what you have to tell people so nobody finds out about your being a fairy. That's what the book said.''

"*What* book?''

"You know. The one where you became real so you could help save Celia from the trolls.''

"Oh, right.'' She vaguely recalled thumbing through that one, marveling that her sister had kept her occupation a secret from the family for so long. Especially considering she'd used every last one of them as characters in her books. "My brother was one of the trolls.'' And her father a king, heaven help Jacq's mythical world.

"He's a troll?'' River asked, clearly awestruck.

J.J. wished she could have bitten off her tongue. "Not a *real* troll. I meant——"

The rag doll was clutched closer. "I don't have any brothers. But if I did, I wouldn't want them to be trolls.''

J.J. nodded in perfect understanding. "It can be a

problem.'' Almost as much a problem as her current predicament. "Listen, River. We need to talk about this. Your dad is really mad at me."

"That's because he doesn't believe in fairies. He doesn't want to get married, either. That's why I wished."

"You made a wish?"

"Uh-huh. The wish you came to give me."

"The one about having a mother?"

"Yes." River fingered the doll's black yarn head, carefully straightening each individual strand so the "hair" fell in a tidy curtain. "I wished for a mother just like you."

It took J.J. a moment to respond. For some odd reason, her throat had closed over, emotions she'd always been able to control with ease fighting for release. She didn't understand it. She'd always lived a practical life. Always made the reasonable choices. Never wished on a star or dreamed of flying to the moon on gossamer wings. That had been her sister's department.

J.J. closed her eyes, admitting the painful truth. She'd always longed for such a rich fantasy life. Longed—just once—to be the creative, head-in-the-clouds daughter. Unfortunately her older sister had filled that role, and quite capably, too.

Taking a deep breath, she faced her tiny nemesis. "Sweetheart, that's why I'm here. I've been sent to explain that your wish isn't possible."

Tears spiked the lashes around River's pale blue eyes and her chin quivered ever so slightly. "You can't stay? You can't be my mommy?"

Oh, great. She'd made the kid cry. Sierra would have her head. "I can give you another wish," she offered out of sheer desperation. "But not...not the one you made."

"I don't want another wish! I want you. I want you

for my mommy. All the other girls have one. All except me. I asked Daddy, but he said no. And Ge—'' She clutched the doll tighter, practically squeezing the stuffing out of it. "Somebody said I could get a mom if I wished. So, I did. I wished real, real hard. That's why you're here. Don't you remember?" Her voice rose. "You have to remember!"

"I'm here to give you a wish, just not—"

"Be my mommy!" River's voice broke. "That's my wish."

J.J. stood there, achingly erect. How fitting. She'd gone from a woman without fantasies of her own, to a breaker of dreams. A destroyer of illusions. A practical twenty-six-year-old who'd never made a wish and who, apparently, couldn't grant one, either. "I'm so sorry, River," she whispered. "What you ask isn't possible."

"Why?" The question was heartrending, dredged from the deepest part of a small child. It was a plea for someone to explain the capricious nature of Fate, to explain why *she* must go without a mother's love.

"I don't know. I've been told I can't do it."

"But *why* can't you?"

A vague memory sparked an idea, something she recalled reading in one of Jacq's books. Clearly using facts as an argument wasn't working. So, perhaps the fantasy laws of her sister's make-believe world would do the trick. J.J. knelt beside River and gathered her close. "You think I'm a fairy, don't you?" At the little girl's nod, she asked, "Can fairies stay people forever?"

"No. Only a little while."

"So how can a fairy be your mother?"

It was obviously a question that hadn't occurred to River. J.J. pressed home her advantage, hating that she was still playing into fantasies instead of dealing with the realities of the situation. "It wouldn't work, sweetie. That's why I have to give you another wish. But," she hastened to add, "it has to be a wish I can do." The way her luck had been running, River would ask to see the dragon. And somehow she doubted Mathias would make an adequate substitution.

"I just wanted a mommy," River whispered. "I don't have any other wishes."

J.J. didn't doubt it. She'd bet her last penny that Raven took care of every need the little girl had. Well...except one. She enclosed River in a warm hug. "I'm so sorry. This is the very first wish I've ever tried to give someone and I'm sorry I can't do it."

"Would you...would you be my mommy if you could?"

The question brought tears to J.J.'s eyes. "I'd love to have a daughter just like you. Any mother would." She felt tiny fingers gently comb through her hair. It was a tentative touch, wistful and delicate, almost instantly withdrawn—a child hesitant to reach for what she wanted most in the world. Was she afraid it might disappear? The thought hurt unbearably.

Easing back, J.J. captured River's chin with the knuckle of her index finger. What incredible eyes the little girl had, as clear and deep as a fast-tumbling stream. Hope and despair were mirrored in the silver-blue depths and J.J. couldn't bring herself to crush that tiny spark of hope. She knew Raven wanted her to shatter his daughter's fantasies, to explain that fairies weren't real. But she couldn't be so brutal. She just couldn't.

"I can't be your mother, River. I'm very sorry about that. If you'll make another wish, I'll try to give it to you—if it's within my powers. Okay?"

"I want you," River tried one last time.

"I'm sorry."

The door opened just then and Raven stood there. River took one look at her father and burst into tears. "She can't do it," the little girl sobbed. "She can't be

my mommy.'' With that, she ripped free of J.J.'s arms
and flung herself into her father's embrace.

Raven cradled his daughter close, his cold black gaze
coming to rest on J.J. A multitude of threats glittered
within those dark depths and she shivered, waiting for
him to rip into her. But to her utter amazement, he simply said, ''Please leave.''

Without another word, she picked up the book she'd
given River and set it on his desk. And then she left.

J.J. couldn't ever recall being more frustrated. Tracking
down River Sierra had proven fairly simple. When she'd
landed in Denver, she'd called in to Blackstone's and
spoken to Gem. The computer had been quite helpful,
providing the address to Raven's office building. Except
for that one useful tidbit, J.J. had been stonewalled ever
since—stonewalled by a computer, no less.

For the fifth time in the past two hours she phoned
Mathias only to be greeted by Gem's now-annoying
electronic voice. Not only did the computer reign su-
preme at Blackstone's, but Jacq—in her infinite wis-
dom—now had the computer taking care of phone duties
at home, too. Perhaps she'd made the switch because of
her pregnancy. Her baby was due in less than a month.
J.J. sighed. Well, it was better than unplugging the
darned thing, which had been Jacq's previous method of
dealing with a phone she didn't want to answer—though
not by much.

''GOOD    EVENING.    YOU'VE    REACHED
BLACKSTONE'S. HOW MAY I HELP YOU?''

''It's J.J. again.''

''GOOD EVENING, MS.—''

''Don't talk, just listen. I don't want any more argu-
ments. I want to speak to Mathias and I want to speak
to him now.''

''MR. BLACKSTONE IS UNAVAILABLE,'' came

the standard retort. "PLEASE STATE NATURE OF PROBLEM."

"I've already told you. The nature of my problem is fulfilling River Sierra's wish." J.J. took a deep breath, struggling to control her temper. "Her father is furious with me. River thinks I'm the fairy out of Jacq's book. And the wish she wants is impossible. What am I supposed to do?"

"YOU ARE TO GRANT WISH OF RIVER SIERRA. PLEASE REFER TO INSTRUCTIONS ON MEMO."

J.J. gritted her teeth. "Haven't you been paying attention? She wants me to be her mother. In case you didn't know, the only way I can do that is by marrying Raven Sierra."

"AFFIRMATIVE. YOU ARE TO GRANT WISH OF RIVER SIERRA."

"Affirmative? Oh, no. That's not an affirmative. Have you lost your mind?" What was she saying? She had to quit acting as if this piece of hardware had the human capacity of thought. "Listen, Gem. I am *not* going to marry Raven Sierra. I'm quite certain that isn't why Mathias sent me."

"YOUR ASSIGNMENT IS SPECIFIC. YOU ARE TO GRANT WISH OF RIVER SIERRA."

She groaned, wondering for the umpteenth time why she was sitting in a hotel room in Denver arguing over the phone with a stupid machine. "Would you please connect me with Mathias so I can discuss the situation directly with him?"

"MR. BLACKSTONE UNAVAILABLE FOR DISCUSSION. PLEASE CONTINUE WITH ASSIGNMENT."

"When will Mathias be available?"

"INFORMATION UNAVAILABLE."

She was getting heartily sick of hearing that particular

refrain. If this was a test, it was a damned annoying one. "How do I contact him?"

"LEAVE MESSAGE OR SEND E-MAIL REPORT."

"Fine. I'll file a report after I hang up. In the meantime, give Mathias a message."

"RELAY MESSAGE."

She thrust her hair behind one ear and shouted into the receiver. "Help!" For a minute she wondered if she'd blown Gem's auditory circuitry. Not that she cared. If they had to fix the machine because it had blown a few fuses, maybe a "real" person would answer the darned phone. Lowering her voice, she continued, "That's it. Just that one word. But you give it to him in large block letters, italicized and underlined three times. You got that?"

"AFFIRMATIVE."

"Just out of curiosity… Does Mathias know what the kid wants? He can't have realized she'd wished for a mother."

"INFORMATION—"

"Yeah, yeah. I know. Information unavailable. Thanks a lot, Gem. You've been a big help."

Apparently sarcasm wasn't a form of communication the computer recognized. "YOU'RE WELCOME, MS. RANDELL," came the dulcet reply. "HAVE A NICE DAY."

With that, Gem broke the connection. J.J. continued to sit on the edge of the bed, fighting for calm. None of this made any sense. Not the assignment. Not River's wish. Not Mathias's demand that she fulfill that wish. He couldn't have known the nature of the little girl's request. When she told him, he'd be suitably appalled and order her directly home. Wouldn't he?

Visions of her father's past manipulations spiked her memory. She'd never known anyone quite as determined to get what he wanted as her father. His reputation for ruthlessness was legendary. It didn't matter what the cost. His personal goals superseded everything.

So, what about Mathias? Perhaps he had more in common with Turk Randell than she'd thought. Instantly she shook her head. No. He wasn't anything like Turk. She drew a ragged breath, struggling to convince herself she hadn't been made a fool of for all these months. Her brother-in-law would never pull the type of stunts her father had. Sure, Mathias had exposed Jacq's secret identity. But there'd been a good reason for that. Right? Just as there must be a good reason for her current dilemma.

A knock at the door reported through the room like a gunshot.

It caught J.J. by surprise and she leapt to her feet, her heart pounding. For a split second she wondered if perhaps the reporters had found her. They certainly were a tenacious bunch. Crossing to the peephole as quietly as she could, she peeked through the opening and saw Raven standing on the other side of the door. For an instant, she was tempted to ignore him. Not that he'd let her get away with it. Like Turk, he'd find a solution to his problem—one guaranteed to work to his advantage. In fact, it wouldn't surprise her if he'd already gotten hold of a key to her room just to cover that particular contingency.

Resisting the urge to straighten her clothing and run a brush through her hair, she unlatched the door and tugged it open. Uh-oh. The warrior had returned. She could see it in his stance, in the light of battle flaming in his black gaze. "Mr. Sierra," she greeted him with impressive calm. "This is a surprise."

He was alone and had changed from his business suit into jeans and a black chambray shirt. Not that it mattered. Whether casual or dressed for success, the man commanded instant attention. With the possible exception of Mathias, she'd never known anyone more capable of instantly dominating any given situation. Not even Turk.

"May I come in?" Raven asked.

She debated for a whole two seconds. The fact that he didn't automatically shoulder his way past decided it for her. "Sure."

Stepping back, she waved him in, wishing she'd taken a spare minute to slip into her heels so they'd be on a more equal level. Barefoot, her five foot nine looked tiny beside his six foot two plus boot heels. Unfortunately she'd kicked her pumps under the bed. And as badly as she wanted them gracing her feet instead of the floor, there was no way she'd treat Raven to a view of her scrambling around on the carpet in search of them.

He removed his leather jacket and tossed it across one of the chairs. Unable to help herself, J.J. eyed the width of his shoulders and the strong muscular back flexing beneath the soft cotton. How could she possibly have failed to notice such an impressive frame? A businessman with the build of a laborer. It was a dangerous combination.

The purely feminine reaction caught her off guard, perhaps because it had been so long since she'd looked at a man that way. Drawing on every ounce of poise, she schooled her expression to hide her reaction, though nothing calmed the hum of excitement racing through her veins.

Raven turned to face her. "You're not surprised I'm here."

"Actually I am," she said easily, pleased that her self-control hadn't completely deserted her. "How did you find me?"

He lifted a winged eyebrow. "Gem gave me the info. I'd assumed you'd left it with her."

She hadn't and J.J. took a moment to mull over the

implications. This was the second time Sierra Consortium's computer unit betrayed more knowledge than should be part of its programming. The possibility that the Gem system at Blackstone's was exchanging information with Raven's unit struck her yet again. But she immediately discarded the notion as ridiculous. There must be built-in safeguards against such a possibility. Still... She'd make a mental note to ask Mathias to look into it—assuming she ever reached the man.

"Would you like a drink?" she asked Raven, indicating the minifridge. "I assume it's fully stocked." After this meeting, she'd do more than assume. She'd find out for certain, and if it was loaded, she'd indulge in one of those pricey little hundred-proof bottles. She'd probably need it after the coming battle.

"I'll pass, thanks. I didn't come to exchange social pleasantries."

Lovely. No doubt Mr. Warrior Man had come to threaten her some more. She indicated the chair he'd used as a coatrack. "Have a seat." She didn't phrase it as a request.

His eyebrow tilted upward again. "A directive, Ms. Randell?"

"Yes, Mr. Sierra. It was." Seated, they'd be on a more equal footing. Standing—even in his current stance lounging against the dresser—gave him far too aggressive a presence.

For the first time, a hint of a smile creased his bronzed face. Inclining his head, he snagged his jacket from the chair and moved it to the end of the bed. Then he sat, his long, lean legs thrust out in front of him. She had a choice. She could either climb over him and take the only other available chair or she could perch on the end of the bed beside his jacket. Neither option appealed. Instead she took up his former stance, resting a hip on the dresser and folding her arms across her chest.

His smile grew to a grin. "Comfortable?"

"Absolutely." She waited a beat, then asked, "So, why have you come?"

His smile faded. "You know damned well why."

She hated conversations that started this way. "I don't suppose you'd care to refresh my memory?"

"You were supposed to tell my daughter you couldn't give her a wish. Does that help your recollection, Ms. Randell?"

"I did precisely what you requested. I told her I wasn't a fairy—not that she believed me. I told her I couldn't be her mother—"

"And you said you'd give her another wish." He straightened abruptly, his booted feet hitting the carpet with a thud. "Why would you do such a thing?"

Ah. So, that was it. "It only seemed fair."

"Fair? I don't give a damn about fair. You were to explain to River that you couldn't give her a wish. And I told you to make it clear that you're not some sort of fairy sent to be her mother. Then you were supposed to hightail it out of there."

"I tried—"

"Not hard enough. Instead she still thinks you're a fairy, still wants you for her mother and is desperate to come up with another wish. A wish you offered. If I'd known you were going to pull a stunt like that, I'd never have let you speak to her alone."

"I did my best," J.J. argued. "I tried to tell her I wasn't a fairy, but she didn't believe me. What more was I expected to do?"

"Tell her fairies aren't real. Explain that it's all make-believe."

Her mouth tightened and she met his glare head-on. Years of practice dealing with domineering men came to her aid. "Mr. Sierra, if you want to destroy your daughter's fantasies, feel free. But I'm not going to do it for you. I gave her a second wish because she was so crushed by my refusal to fulfill her first one.''

"And what if she asks for something as impossible as before?"

"I warned her it would have to be something I could do. And trust me, marrying you isn't on that list, no matter how badly your daughter could use a mother.''

She'd gone too far. Slowly he gained his feet, his face falling into steely lines. "Don't push me, Ms. Randell. You won't like the results.''

J.J. lifted her chin, refusing to be intimidated. "Don't threaten me, Mr. Sierra. I don't want to disappoint your daughter, but if you don't back down, I'll simply leave. Then you can deal with River's fantasies in your own inimitable fashion.''

"I'm tempted to take you up on that offer.''

"Feel free. If I weren't so concerned about River, I'd have already left.''

"You're not going anywhere until we've straightened out this mess.'' His tone didn't leave room for any doubt. "Tomorrow you're coming to the office and share a pleasant lunch with my daughter. At that point she's going to make another wish—a wish you *can* fulfill. And then, fairy lady, you're to fly back to Seattle. I don't care if it's by wing or by plane, but you're leaving and not returning. Ever. You got that?''

She clenched her teeth so hard she couldn't believe they didn't crack. "Oh, you've made yourself crystal clear,'' she assured, once she could speak again.

"Excellent. Now, it's time for some answers. Why does Blackstone want this procurement so badly? Is it for his wife? Is he really willing to tick me off over such a trifle?''

"I have no idea what you're talking about.'' *Why* didn't he sit down again? She hated being at such a disadvantage. She slid her hip off the dresser and straightened, knowing full well her posture was far too defensive—arms folded across her chest, spine ramrod stiff, chin tilted to an aggressive angle. It was a dead giveaway to someone like Raven, but she couldn't help that. She felt defensive. "What procurement?"

"Don't play the innocent, Ms. Randell. It doesn't suit you."

She knew her appearance made playing the ingenue a bit of a stretch, but that wasn't her fault. Genetics had given her a tall, slim build, sloe-brown eyes and an over-all exotic look. She'd become accustomed to men making assumptions. That didn't mean she liked it. And on a certain level, having Raven Sierra make the same mistake came as a severe disappointment. She'd have thought him a shrewder judge of character.

She lowered her eyes to hide the disillusionment that must be reflected there. Why should this man be any different than those she'd known in the past? she chastised herself. No doubt he thought women were either saints, whores or children. It didn't take a mental giant to figure out which category he'd assigned to her.

Gathering her composure, she swept all hint of emotion from her expression and lifted her gaze to meet his. "I don't really care whether or not you believe me. And I refuse to get into an argument over my veracity."

"Or lack thereof."

Her mouth tugged to one side and she inclined her head. "Touché. But I'm telling you—flat-out—that until I received that memo today I'd never even heard of you or your daughter. If Mathias had prior dealings with you, he never informed me of them."

He studied her for a few seconds before nodding. "Fair enough."

"Now would you please tell me what this is about?"

"I'm surprised you haven't called Blackstone and asked."

Ouch. Point scored. "I haven't been able to get through to him," she admitted reluctantly.

"How convenient."

"Let's stop dancing around, shall we?" Annoyance seeped into her voice. "I'm here to give your daughter a Christmas wish."

"An October Christmas wish."

She released her breath in a noisy sigh. "Fine. An October Christmas wish. That's it. End of agenda. You suspect there's more to it than that. Why?"

"I don't suspect. I know."

"Then perhaps you'd enlighten me. You claim Mathias used this wish as an excuse to send me here and blackmail you into giving him... What?" She tilted her head to one side. "What is he so desperate to get that he'd create this whole ridiculous scenario in order to gain it?"

"Okay. We'll play the game your way. You want to know what he wants?"

"Please. I don't think I can stand the anticipation."

Unlike Gem, he caught her sarcasm. "It's quite simple, Ms. Randell. He'd like to purchase a painting I own."

"A painting?"

"A very special one."

She stared at him uneasily. "Would you care to be more specific?"

"Sure. It's a painting of a naked fairy riding a butterfly." His fathomless dark eyes mocked her. "It's a painting of you, Ms. Randell. And for some reason, your brother-in-law's determined to get his hands on it. Now why is that, do you suppose? Why would he go to such extremes to buy back a painting his wife auctioned off last Christmas?"

He'd struck an unexpected blow. "You bought—"

She fought for breath and tried again. "*You* bought the painting?"

"As a birthday present for my daughter. And just so you know, it's not for sale. Not at any price."

"And Mathias has been trying to buy it back?"

"Supposedly for his wife. Or so he claims." Bitter cynicism tainted his gaze as he eyed her. "Though I'm beginning to have my doubts."

The implication hit hard, igniting a fury so hot and fierce she trembled with it. "Get out."

He continued to study her for an impossible few seconds. Then he exhaled heavily. "I'm wrong about that much, aren't I?" he finally said. "I apologize. I shouldn't have jumped to conclusions."

"Apology accepted. Now get out."

He reached for her, his movement as slow and cautious as though she were a wounded animal. Gently he captured her chin in his palm, his long fingers splaying across the smooth expanse of her cheek, sparking a line of fire that burned her skin as if it were a brand. "I'm sorry," he repeated. "That was uncalled for. You didn't deserve that."

Oh, great. Now she was going to cry. How could one man succeed in rousing such a riot of conflicting emotions? she wondered in despair. One minute they were fierce enemies, pitched in a no-holds-barred battle. And in the next they were comrades, exhausted soldiers who'd fought too many wars and licked too many wounds. Warriors who wanted to curl up in each others' arms for a brief respite, safe from those who would hurt them.

It took a moment to steady her voice enough to reply. "Mathias is my brother-in-law, not my lover."

"I know that now. I apologize for insulting you. It won't happen again."

The fiery anger eased, shifting to something else

equally fiery, something that worried her far more than false assumptions or Christmas wishes run amuck. She suddenly realized that Raven's breathing had quickened, an exact match for her own. He stroked her cheek with gentle fingertips and the fire raged hotter. And his eyes, those brilliant black eyes of his... A weary understanding dawned in that dark gaze—an understanding she wanted desperately to deny.

"Damn," he whispered. Ever so carefully, he released her, his hand slipping away. He stepped back, allowing her to breathe again. With an economy of motion, he recovered his jacket from the end of the bed and crossed to the door.

"Noon tomorrow, fairy lady," he reminded her without looking around. "Don't be late."

And then he was gone leaving her more upset and confused than ever. She wrapped her arms around her waist, trying to hug away the pain. It didn't help. What in the hell had she gotten herself into? she wondered anxiously. And what in the world could she do to fight her way free?

River opened the book Justice had given her. "Read it again, Gem," she demanded. She'd already listened to the story four times. But it was so wonderful, she had to hear it once more.

"READING TIME EXPIRED TWO POINT THREE MINUTES AGO. LIGHTS MUST NOW BE EXTINGUISHED FOR SLEEP PERIOD."

"I don't want to go to bed."

"ERROR NUMBER THREE-OH-EIGHT."

"I know. I know." River pouted. "That means I have to go to bed, right?"

"AFFIRMATIVE."

"Okay." She tucked the book carefully under her pillow. "But turn on my night-light."

"NIGHT-LIGHT ACTIVATED."

"Gem?"

"STATE REQUEST."

"Will you read me the book again, so I can go to sleep? I won't look at the pictures. I promise. I just want to hear the story."

"AFFIRMATIVE. BOOK HAS BEEN SCANNED INTO MEMORY."

"Gem?"

"CONTINUE."

"Do you think the book is right? Do you think Fausta's magic would work?"

"INSUFFICIENT DATA TO FORMULATE CONCLUSION."

"Huh?"

"IT IS NOT POSSIBLE TO DETERMINE OUTCOME WITHOUT MORE INFORMATION."

"You don't know?"

"AFFIRMATIVE."

"Do you think we could try? It would be like the birthday wish. Maybe it works like that."

"AFFIRMATIVE. FOLLOWING REQUIRED STEPS SHOULD RESULT IN DESCRIBED OUTCOME."

River yawned. "What does that mean?"

"MAGIC SHOULD WORK."

"Okay, good. Let's start tomorrow." She snuggled deeper under the covers. "Will you help?"

"AFFIRMATIVE."

"Thanks." She hugged her rag doll and closed her eyes. "I love you, Gem."

"ONE MOMENT. PROCESSING." A confused series of beeps emitted from the speakers. "RELAYING INFORMATION TO PRIMARY FOR DIRECTION. REQUEST ANALYSIS AND INSTRUCTION."

But by the time the analysis had been completed and

the instructions returned, River was sound asleep. If she heard the computer's whisper-mode response, it was only in a dream.

"GEM UNIT LOVES FEMALE OFFSPRING UNIT, TOO."

had not known existed, River was going away. If she heard the computer's distant, tinny response, it was only in a dream.

GLANDES AND LOVE ISSUED A QUARTER CHALLENGE.

## CHAPTER THREE

"What you've requested is very difficult and very, very dangerous," Fausta explained. "And the price is high. But if you're willing to risk everything, your wish is possible. The first task you must accomplish is to gather seven gifts for Nemesis."

Justice nodded, struggling to be brave. Fortunately her desire far outweighed her fear. "What's the first gift?" she asked.

"It's a simple one," Fausta said with a smile. "You must take a tiny piece of love and slip it into a silken bag."

Page 13, *The Great Dragon Hunt*
by Jack Rabbitt

"DAMMIT all! What the hell did I do with my cuff links?"

"You're not supposed to use bad words," River reminded.

Raven released his breath in a gusty sigh. She was right, of course. When Maise had died, he'd sat in a darkened room, holding a tiny infant in his arms and vowed to be the perfect parent. Foolish of him. He should have realized perfection would come hard to a man so riddled with imperfections. Still, he continued to battle his less noble inclinations. Too bad success came in such varying degrees—as providence seemed determined to prove this morning. His mouth twisted. Not to mention last night.

"Sorry, honey. I'll try to be more careful." He frowned at his dresser. "I just don't know what the, er—" he spared a quick glance in his daughter's direction "—*heck* I did with those cuff links. I could have sworn I left them right here."

"I lose things all the time, too." She clutched her rag doll protectively to her chest, as though to prevent such a disastrous fate from befalling her most prized possession. "Maybe it was pixies. They like to play tricks on people."

"It wasn't pixies," he stated forcefully. Making an effort to moderate his voice, he added, "You know there's no such thing."

"Nawna said there was. They used to steal her glasses all the time. Then she'd say, 'Dang pixies. I'm pix'lated, I am.'"

Her imitation was nearly perfect. Quite a feat considering the old woman had been gone a full year now. "Nawna liked to play pretend. When she told you about the pixies and the fairies and all that other sh—er—*stuff*, she was playing make-believe. They're not real."

His daughter simply looked at him with childlike stubbornness and he sighed again, giving it up. He knew a fruitless battle when he saw one. He opened his dresser drawer and shoved aside a pile of socks. Damn. Still no cuff links. What the hell had he done with them? "They were the cuff links you picked out for my birthday," he explained, opening another drawer. "That's why I feel so bad about misplacing them."

"It's okay. I'm not mad." Tilting her head to one side, she fixed him with the sweet eyes of a dreamer. "Do you want me to wish for them back?"

Raven gritted his teeth, swallowing the curses burning to be vented. "No, thanks. Why don't you save that wish for yourself."

"Okay." She ground a toe into the thick carpet, studying the impression it left behind. Apparently satisfied with the results, she returned her attention to her father. "Will Justice be coming for a visit today?"

"Yes. She promised to come for lunch."

Assuming he hadn't frightened her off. Somehow he doubted he had. J.J. Randell didn't strike him as the type to frighten easily. Of course, that business right before he left might have given her second thoughts. He shook his head in disgust. Why the hell had he insulted her, anyway? Self-preservation, probably. There was something about River's fairy lady that disturbed him—disturbed him in ways he hadn't experienced in years.

He scowled as he analyzed the problem. What was it? What had affected him on such an intensely primitive level? Perhaps it had been the way she'd trembled when he'd touched her, or the pain and disillusionment darkening her honey brown eyes, a pain and disillusionment that mirrored his own. He only knew that the instant he'd felt the sweet silk of her cheek beneath his hand, he'd wanted to back her up the two steps it would have taken to reach the bed. And then he'd wanted to make love to her, to transform her anguish to pleasure, to release the seething emotions she kept under such tight control.

Instead he'd walked out the door—probably the only smart move he'd made since meeting her.

"Daddy?" River tugged on his pants leg, crumpling the material. Not that he cared. He sort of liked going to work with little girl crumples creasing the perfect cut of his suit. It kept him grounded. "Daddy, why can't we see Justice now?"

"Because I invited her for lunch, not breakfast. We're going to talk about your wish while we eat and see if we can't get that taken care of today."

For a brief instant River brightened. "Are you going to make her stay and be my mommy?"

"She can't do that, remember?"

"Because she's a fairy and fairies can't stay people or they die. Right?"

"J.J. isn't a fairy. Fairies aren't real." It was a refrain he'd repeated a hundred times. It had as much impact on this occasion as it had the other ninety-nine. Usually his daughter simply ignored the repetitive assertion. This time she chose to counter it.

"If she's not a fairy then why can't she be my mommy?"

"Because—" Her logic defeated him. Where the hell did she come up with this stuff? If he didn't know better, he'd swear someone was feeding her the appropriate questions to ask. "Because she'd have to marry me. And for two people to get married, they have to love each other."

"Like you and mommy did?"

His throat grew tight. "Yeah, sweetheart. Just like that."

"I could wish that you and Justice fall in love. Okay?"

Uh-oh. "Don't go there, River. It won't work."

"Because Justice is a fairy?"

"Justice is make-believe. J.J. is a real person. And I'm not in love with either one. Love can't be wished into existence. It has to grow on its own." He waited for his daughter to cite another Jack Rabbitt "truism" to counter his statement. To his utter relief, she simply nodded.

"Okay. I won't make that my wish."

"River, J.J. isn't a fairy," he tried one final time. "Got it? You need to trust me about that."

"Grown-ups never believe in magic stuff. They're not supposed to 'cuz it's only for kids." River trotted to the door and paused. She'd lifted her rag doll to her shoulder so that only her eyes peeked over the black yarn head. He groaned. Heaven protect him from the power of those glorious eyes. "Only fairies can give wishes, Daddy. That's how come I know Justice is a real fairy."

A touch of indulgence colored her piping voice and he could have sworn her gaze held a spark of amusement far exceeding a child of five. It was positively frightening. He also suspected it was a hint of what he could expect in the years ahead. Satisfied at having delivered the final salvo regarding fantasy lore, River slipped from the room leaving Raven to consign J.J., Jack Rabbitt and Mathias Blackstone to the darkest pits of purgatory.

And he did it using words his daughter would find quite objectionable.

She'd made a mistake. J.J. realized it the instant she stepped foot in Raven's office. She'd deliberately dressed all in black, having purchased her current outfit just two short hours ago. In the store, the plain calf-length black skirt and equally plain black sweater had seemed simple and unassuming. Only one small detail had escaped her calculations.

It hadn't occurred to her that Raven would dress in black, too. She shook her head in disgust. Good grief! With their matching dark hair and eyes, they looked like mated bookends. He must have thought the same, for his attention fastened on her with a sharp, intimate awareness. And with that single look, memories of the previous night stormed her defenses.

Unable to help herself, her gaze fastened on his hands,

remembering how he'd touched her. It had been such a light, delicate touch for such long, powerful hands. And his shoulders... She'd been fascinated by the taut play of corded sinew and muscles beneath his chambray shirt. Not to mention his eyes, black and hard and glittering with passion. She could even recall his varying scents, the woodsy aroma of his cologne combined with the alluring sweetness of his breath when he'd apologized. If circumstances had been different...

Reality crashed in on her. Oh, no! This would never do. How could she have allowed herself to become so distracted? Gathering every ounce of self-control, she met his amused gaze. "Want me to call next time for a wardrobe check?" she asked, cocking an inquisitive eyebrow. "It's so embarrassing to wear the same outfit, isn't it?"

His mouth pulled to one side and he released a low, rumbling laugh. "Good idea. Although, I didn't realize fairies favored black—when they chose to wear clothes, that is."

If he thought to embarrass her, he'd soon find it took a lot more than that. Too many trips through hell's fire spared her that ignominy. "No, it's definitely a dragon's color," she replied. "If it weren't for the eyes, you could almost pass for Nemesis."

"Nemesis?"

"The dragon in the latest Jack Rabbitt book. Didn't River show it to you?"

"No."

J.J. shrugged. "It has a dragon on the cover who is, I assume, a major character in the story. I gave it to River before I had a chance to read it, but I know my sister modeled the creature after Mathias. If you'd ever met him, you'd agree it's an uncanny resemblance. Jacq's quite talented."

"Blackstone as a dragon. How appropriate."

She lifted an eyebrow. "Really? I'd have said the same about you."

"Daddy's not a dragon," River announced from the doorway. "He's a real person."

It was too good an opening to resist. "So am I, sweetheart. I'm as real as your dad."

River nodded complacently. "Just until you turn back into a fairy."

"Sweetheart, would you mind coloring while J.J. and I talk?" Raven interrupted. "We won't be long."

River's reluctance was obvious. She ran to J.J.'s side for a quick hug. "Don't leave," she demanded. "Not yet."

"I'll stay right here. I promise."

Apparently satisfied, River crossed to her desk and removed crayons and a pad of paper. Raven waited until his daughter became absorbed in her art project, before murmuring, "You're not going to win with her on this fairy business. She's got an answer for everything."

"Thanks to my sister. According to River, book number three has Justice turning into a human for a short time." J.J. slanted him a wry look. "Bet you didn't know they had rules about these things."

"No, I didn't, though I'm learning." He folded his arms across his chest, his droll tone a perfect match for hers. "One of these days I'm gonna thank your sister in person for inventing such an interesting storyline."

She chuckled. "You'll have to go through Mathias to do that. Try it and you'll see why Jacq used him as a model for her dragon."

"Ah, but a minute ago you were calling me a dragon."

Raven leaned closer—far too close. Once again, it brought back memories of the night before—memories she'd just as soon suppress. Unfortunately, that option wasn't available to her. He instantly dominated, eclipsing every other sight and sound. Unable to help herself, she gathered in his now-familiar scent—the hint of cedar with an underlining tang of spice. Finally she glanced at him, losing herself in the unrelenting blackness of his gaze.

"Do you think Mathias could stop me from getting what I wanted?" His breath fanned her lips and she drew that in as well. "Do you really think I'd allow it?"

Did she? Instinctively she sensed that a battle between the two men wouldn't be a pleasant occurrence. Both were powerful, both fighting for what they loved most in the world. No. She wouldn't care to guess the potential outcome of such a confrontation. It would be far better if she found a way to ease matters out between the two of them.

She lowered her voice, hoping to keep River from overhearing their discussion. "Jacq has given your daughter nothing but pleasure. Why would you want to harm someone who's done everything she could to bring joy into childrens' lives?"

"She's filled River's head with fantasies," came the biting retort. "Dangerous fantasies."

"Fantasies found in books you purchased for your daughter," J.J. couldn't resist pointing out.

She'd hit on a sore point and his mouth compressed. "True," he conceded. "But your sister also committed one other unforgivable sin."

"And what is that?"

"She brought *you* into our lives. And you're trouble, fairy lady. Serious trouble."

So was he. Trouble to her peace of mind and emotional stability. His eyes caught fire, burning with an intensity she could practically feel. It splashed across her skin, burrowed deep into her pores and sizzled through her veins. He shouldn't have this sort of effect on her. She should be immune to his type. He wasn't safe.

Men like Raven Sierra needed total control, both in
their lives and in the lives of anyone they touched. She'd
lived with someone like that already—her father. As a
result, she'd made up her mind long ago: The man she
eventually loved would be kind and gentle and easy-
going. Raven couldn't act that way even on his best day.

Still, his allure drew her. Potent and dangerous, it
tempted, speaking to her on some forbidden, primitive
level. J.J. struggled to check her reaction to him. When
she'd worked for her father's PR firm, she'd dealt with
any number of difficult clients. One of the reasons she'd
been so successful handling them was her ability to dis-
engage her emotions. They never touched her—not
physically and never, ever emotionally. Somehow she
suspected it would be far more difficult to hold Raven
at a safe distance should he choose to force the issue.
Look at how it had gone the night before.

"It's happening again, isn't it?" he murmured.

Honesty compelled her to admit the truth. "Yes. It
doesn't make sense, does it?"

"Not a bit."

He shifted closer and more than anything she wanted
to experience his touch again, feel the slide of his hand
along her skin. "Why did you invite me here today?"
she whispered in despair. "I thought it was to try to
straighten out this mess. Or was it actually so you could
seduce me?"

"And if it was?"

She'd fall—her defenses breached, her guard
dropped—she'd surrender. She closed her eyes. She was
so tired of fighting. She needed solace, not another skir-
mish. "What do you want, Raven?"

With a sigh, he eased back, helping to bank the fire's
heat. "As tempting as the thought, seducing you wasn't
my intention."

"Did you invite me so you could threaten my family?"

"No need to waste my day threatening your family. I can do that any old time."

For an instant, she thought he was serious. Then she caught a glitter of what could only be amusement in those impossibly dark eyes. A slow smile built across the taut planes of his face, easing the rigid control she'd seen up till now. Heaven help her, but he was a gorgeous man when he relaxed his defenses.

She took a deep breath. Then another. To her relief, she'd regained some semblance of control. It would seem the battle hadn't been lost after all. At least…not yet. "Why, Mr. Sierra, I'm shocked. Surely that's not a sense of humor you're revealing?" she dared to tease.

"A fatal flaw I haven't quite eradicated," came the gentle response.

She allowed herself the luxury of a chuckle. "Ah. That explains it. Well, never fear. With your determination I'm sure you'll succeed before long."

"I appreciate your confidence."

His response sounded as dry as hers. Once again they were two experienced and wary warriors, their instinct for self-preservation preventing them from doing much more than parry easy blows as they cautiously circled. If she dared lower her guard again, would he attack? Her mouth tugged to one side. No doubt about it. He'd aim his assault at any perceived weakness, just as her father had taught her to do.

So far, she hadn't identified any holes in his armor—other than his daughter. But her own weakness was all too easy to spot. It centered on his attention-snagging, heart-stopping smile and encompassed everything from fathomless black eyes to broad, protective shoulders to lean hips and well-used cowboy boots. She found such an unexpected desire as unnerving as it was impossible and could only hope he didn't notice before she had a chance to rebuild some seriously impaired defenses.

"Shall we get this show on the road?" she suggested.

"In a minute." He frowned—not a good sign, she'd come to learn. "Have you seen this morning's paper?"

"No." Clothing had been her priority when she awoke. "I had an errand to run and didn't have an opportunity to read it."

Raven crossed to his desk, opened a drawer and removed a folded section of paper. He spun it across the glass surface. J.J. approached, dismayed to see a photo of the three of them from the previous day. Raven dominated the shot. He held River cradled close and had his other arm slung around J.J.'s shoulder in a protective embrace. She was looking up at him, her expression an alarming combination of entreaty and confusion. The poor, helpless woman being rescued by the big, tough man. Just great.

Of course, the worst part was the headline. "Mystery Woman Touches Mr. Untouchable Where It Counts," ran the lurid commentary. Beneath the photo, in large block letters it read, "Can you identify this woman?"

"Do you think they've found out who I am?" she asked uneasily.

"Not yet. But it's only a matter of time."

He was right and J.J. ran through the most likely scenarios that would occur when someone eventually placed her. First, they'd run a background check. After that, it wouldn't take much for the reporters to discover her engagement to Raven was bogus. With a little digging, they might even find out her purpose for being here. And if that happened...

She paled. Mathias wouldn't appreciate the true nature of her assignment being uncovered. If the press ever found out she'd come to dispense Christmas wishes it would lead straight to him. And once it did, people would be all over Blackstone's begging to have their wishes granted.

J.J. thrust the paper back at Raven. "Look. I need to get this business taken care of as quickly and quietly as possible."

His laugh had a harsh, almost bitter ring to it. "No joke, sweetheart. Maybe if you'd realized that yesterday, we wouldn't be in our current predicament."

She spared River a quick glance. The little girl was still at her play area, busily adding to her wall of crayon drawings. "How was I supposed to know the press would be there?" she objected in a heated undertone. "Or that they'd assume we're engaged?"

He leaned across the desk toward her. "It's called discretion." He bit out the words in an equally soft voice. "You scope out a situation before barging right into the middle of it."

"That's what I thought I was doing. I asked for you so we could discuss how you wanted her wish handled. I stood at the back of that mob and waited quietly. Then all of a sudden—" Her eyes narrowed as her memory kicked in. "Wait just one darn minute. This is all your fault," she accused.

"My fault." He shook his head in disbelief. "How do you come up with that one?"

"You…you *looked* at me."

"Looked at you," he repeated, disdain edging his husky tones.

"Stared, in fact." She stabbed her finger at him. "And don't try denying it. I know when I'm being stared at and you were staring. If you hadn't, no one would have paid any attention to my presence there."

"You don't think so?"

"No. Instead you might as well have waved a red flag and shouted, 'Hey, *amigos,* check her out.'"

He released his breath in a slow sigh. "I gather it runs in the family?"

She tried not to let her confusion show. "What?"

"A propensity for overactive imaginations."

He circled the desk and she fell back a step. A hint of grim amusement touched his hard gaze at the telling act. She drew herself up, furious that she'd allowed him to see how profoundly he affected her. She was equally determined he wouldn't catch her off guard again. "I don't have an overactive imagination. In fact, most people would question whether I have any imagination at all."

"Pull the other one, sweetheart. You and that sister of yours are probably so caught up in your little fantasies you wouldn't know reality if it sat up and barked like a dog."

If he only knew! "For your information, I'm the most pragmatic person you'll ever meet."

"Yeah, right. Whatever."

"You think because my sister writes about fairies and trolls and dragons that I'm the same?" she demanded fiercely. "That's totally illogical."

"Who's trying to give a child a Christmas wish in October, Ms. Pragmatic? That hardly falls into the realm of normalcy, now does it?"

"Gee, and here I thought I was being kindhearted," she retorted. "Silly me. But as long as we're on the subject... Since when did having an active imagination or indulging in fantasies rate as a cardinal sin?"

His expression closed over with frightening rapidity, every muscle in his body tensing. She'd scored a direct hit without even realizing there was anything there worth striking. Winter had returned to this particular Sierra mountain. Even his eyes had gone flat and hard, like black ice on tarmac.

"This subject is at an end, Ms. Randell. You've said

you'd like to complete your assignment. I agree. The sooner you leave, the better."

His comment shouldn't hurt. He meant nothing to her, therefore, his opinions shouldn't matter in the least. She turned away. So why did her chest feel tight? And why did she feel precariously close to tears? Ridiculous. She hadn't cried since...

She swallowed. She couldn't remember when she'd last cried. The truth was, she didn't cry. Didn't get her feelings hurt. Didn't feel drawn to untouchable mountain peaks. And she certainly didn't long for impossible fantasies. That was Jacq's providence—one long denied J.J. She was the rational daughter, the practical one, she reminded herself. The rippling pain intensified and she closed her eyes, fighting for strength.

*Focus on your assignment, dammit! Nothing else matters. Nothing.*

She subdued the clamoring of dreams, subdued them with an expertise that came from years of practice. They were far from reach, so it wasn't difficult. At long last, control returned and she lifted her head, focusing on River. "Do you know what her latest wish is?" she questioned calmly.

His eyes narrowed, but he took the change of topic in stride. "She hasn't told me, yet. But I'm hoping we can take care of it over lunch."

J.J. turned to face him. Behind her, she heard River desert her play area and approach. "I'd appreciate that. I didn't come prepared for a lengthy visit. In fact, I'd anticipated returning to Seattle yesterday."

"I don't plan to delay you any further. I want you out of both our lives as soon as possible."

She smiled sweetly. "Gee, thanks."

River tugged at the bottom of his sweater. "Daddy! Don't make her go," she pleaded urgently.

"She's not leaving until she's given you your wish," he reassured.

"Promise?"

"Sure, sweetheart. I promise."

J.J. stirred uneasily. His words had a fateful ring to them. Somehow, she suspected he'd regret ever uttering them.

Worse, she suspected *she'd* regret them even more.

# CHAPTER FOUR

Justice cradled the silk-lined bag to her chest and allowed her laughter to ring out. It raced through the forest, greeting all it found with its happy sound. She'd done it! She'd captured the prince's kiss in her bag, a kiss filled with true love—a love that would last through all of time's trials and tribulations. A love that would grow and strengthen like the magical oak that lived in the very center of Fairy.

Now she had but one final task before the wakening kiss of morning arrived. She slipped into night's embrace and stood beneath the silver rain of moonlight. And there, she thanked the Great Maker for His wondrous gift.

> Page 15, *The Great Dragon Hunt*
> by Jack Rabbitt

"WHERE are we having lunch?" J.J. asked as they left his office.

He spared her a brief glance. "I didn't think it would be safe to go out in public together, so I arranged for lunch to be catered in the executive dining room."

"Smart move."

"I thought so." He paused by his secretary's desk. "Any messages, Mrs. Cruxley?"

"Yes, sir. I'll put them on your desk. There's nothing urgent. Tomorrow's meeting with the board has been moved back two weeks as you requested." She shot J.J. a quick look. "And the gentleman you've been trying to reach is still unavailable."

J.J. bit back a laugh. It didn't take much effort to figure out who that "gentleman" might be. It would seem she wasn't the only one having a tough time getting through to Mathias.

"Also, the…um…research information you requested is available," the secretary continued. "I've typed up the notes. You can access them on your computer."

"Excellent. Have the caterers arrived?"

"Yes, sir. They're in the kitchen now. Lunch should be ready in about fifteen minutes."

"Thank you, Mrs. Cruxley."

They continued down the plush corridor with River dancing between them. She caught hold of first her father's hand, then J.J.'s. To an outsider they undoubtedly looked like the perfect family unit. Another lesson on how deceptive appearances could be.

"What exactly is Sierra Consortium, if you don't mind my asking?" J.J. questioned.

"We're a group of businessmen who own ranches."

By the look of the place it must be a lot of ranches, and all of them doing extremely well. "Cattle?"

"Mostly. We've begun to diversify somewhat over the past few years. But that's our primary focus."

He opened a set of double doors at the end of the hallway. She preceded him into a large, luxurious dining room dominated by a huge table capable of seating at least sixteen. At one end of the room stood an elaborate bar and at the other was a sitting area fronted by a wall of glass. J.J. crossed to that side of the room curious to check out the view.

It was as spectacular as she'd suspected and surprisingly clear. The Rocky Mountains jutted upward against a vivid blue sky, a cap of snow giving the peaks a picture-perfect appearance. How many business deals had been closed here with a drink in one hand, a contract in the other and a sunset painted across snow-topped mountains? More than one, she'd be willing to bet.

Raven approached, the thick carpeting absorbing his footfall. If she hadn't sensed his presence the unexpected sound of his voice would have caught her by surprise. "Something wrong?" he asked.

She decided to answer honestly. "I just wondered how many deals this view helped close."

"Not many. I don't do business with men or women swayed by so little. It means they can be bent just as easily in a different direction by another, more determined party."

Good point. "Then it's not business at all costs?" How unique—and how utterly opposite to her father's approach.

"If that's your philosophy, then your priorities are in a deep hole headin' one way."

She turned, smiling at the phrase. "Straight down?"

"No other direction to go once you've dug yourself in over your head."

"A warning, Mr. Sierra?"

"I believe it is, Ms. Randell." He gestured toward the table. "Why don't we dispense with the formalities for the present and be sociable."

Somehow she doubted he meant sociable in the same way he had last night. "For River's sake?"

He shook his head, the thick black waves of his hair brushing the collar of his suit coat. "Not just hers, but for all our sakes. Time's of the essence and I suspect I'll find it more difficult to lock horns with J.J. than with Ms. Randell."

Perhaps. Unfortunately *she'd* find both Raven and Mr. Sierra equally difficult. She glanced at River who had fixed her intense blue eyes on them. Forcing a smile, J.J. nodded. Why not? Lunch wouldn't take long. And with luck, the wish would now be do-able. She could afford to be gracious for the next few hours. Once through with this particular Christmas wish she'd be in no hurry to request another—which might have been Mathias's goal all along. She couldn't think of any other reason he'd still be unavailable to take her calls—or Raven's, for that matter.

"I think your suggestion is excellent. Raven." His name sat uncomfortably on her tongue.

His mouth twitched. "Thank you. J.J."

"Daddy? Can we sit by the windows and have a picnic?" River requested.

He didn't hesitate. "Excellent idea, pumpkin. It's a perfect day for a picnic."

The caterers had set one end of the expansive table with silver, china and crystal marked with the consortium's logo. In a few expert movements, Raven stripped everything from the mahogany surface and transferred the linen table cloth to an open spot by the windows. J.J. collected the plates, silverware and napkins while River carefully transported the crystal goblets. Once the impromptu "table" had been arranged to her satisfaction, she took her place on the far side, her back to the windows.

"You sit there," she instructed her father, pointing to a spot across from her. "And Justice, you sit next to him."

J.J. started to correct her, then gave it up and dropped to the floor in a graceful swirl of soft black wool. For now, it looked as if she was stuck answering to the fairy's name. A moment later, Raven followed suit, lowering himself to sit cross-legged beside her, perfectly at ease. Now here was a match for Mathias. Like her brother-in-law, Raven was comfortable in any setting, handling any occasion or circumstance with deft authority. She could think of plenty of businessmen who'd have looked like utter fools sitting on the floor of an executive dining room—including her father.

But not Raven.

"Oh! I almost forgot," River exclaimed.

She jumped up and ran back to the table. An instant later she returned, carefully transporting a bowl of flowers and a pair of red candlesticks in cut-glass holders. Once she'd placed them to her satisfaction, Raven reached into his pocket and retrieved a gold lighter, igniting it with a flick of his thumb. Leaning forward, he cupped his hand around the tip of the candles, and applied the flame to each wick.

"What do you think, sweetheart?" he asked. "Is everything how you want it?"

River's eyes shone with pleasure. "It's beautiful. Thank you, Daddy."

A waitress appeared in the doorway leading to the kitchen. Spotting them, she smothered a laugh with her hand before turning to call a soft comment to whomever had accompanied her. A man's head peered around the corner, then vanished. Not the most professional caterers, J.J. thought sourly, which surprised her. She'd have expected Raven to hire only the best.

Straightening a haphazardly set cap on dirt brown hair, the woman approached and J.J. was seized with an odd feeling of familiarity. "Good afternoon, Mr. Sierra," she greeted them cheerfully, shoving an oversize pair of glasses higher on the bridge of her nose. "You ready to eat?"

Raven lifted an eyebrow. "I prefer to see a menu first and place our drink order. Isn't that how you usually operate?"

"Oh, right." She thrust her hands into the pockets of her apron, then into the pockets of her dress. Finally she came up with a pad of paper. Yanking a pencil from behind her ear she hesitated, the lead tip poised above the pad. "What would you like to drink?"

"Mrs. Cruxley put a bottle of Chardonnay in the refrigerator. We'll start with that. River, what would you like, sweetheart?"

"Orange juice, please."

"Coming right up." The waitress glanced at J.J. "Would you care for anything besides the wine, Ms...." She arched a questioning eyebrow.

"Randell. And no. The wine will be fine, thanks."

"Right. I'll bring it along with the menus in just a sec." With a quick smile the waitress hastened back in the direction of the kitchen.

The moment she'd left, River clasped her hands together, trembling with excitement. "Okay, I'm ready to wish," she said, clearly unable to wait any longer to make her big announcement.

J.J. and Raven exchanged quick, uneasy glances. "Remember, it has to be something I can do," she warned.

"I 'member." She closed her eyes and whispered, "I wish... I wish you would be my mommy for our vacation."

Glasses rattled overhead and the waitress's voice cut across River's. "Oops. Sorry to interrupt. I brought your drinks."

"Leave the wine and bring me the bottle of J&B from the wet bar and a glass," Raven bit out, thrusting a hand through his hair. "I'm gonna need it."

"Make that two glasses," J.J. added.

He waited until the waitress left before responding. "No way, River. I said it had to be something we could do. And having J.J. for a mother—"

"A *pretend* mother," she clarified. "Just for our *vacation.*"

"Pick something else. How about a new doll or a trip to the zoo or a puppy?"

"I have a doll and we go to the zoo all the time." She frowned, interlocking her fingers. "I *do* want a puppy, but I want Justice more."

"Choose the puppy, honey," Raven advised. "J.J. is not going to be your mother—real, pretend, or otherwise. And that's final."

"But you promised, Daddy! You did." River leapt to her feet, tears filling her eyes. Skirting the tablecloth, she threw herself into J.J.'s arms. "Didn't he? Fairies always tell the truth. Tell Daddy he promised."

Fairies always tell the truth? J.J. groaned. Just great. One more detail she could thank Jacq for incorporating in her books. "Yes, he did promise. But if you'll remember the wish had to be something I could do."

"Being my mommy for our vacation *is* something you can do."

"Let me guess. It was in the book."

"Not the part about being a mommy," River confessed, obviously trying to be a good little fairy.

"But being a human for a while was, is that it?"

The little girl nodded, swiping at the tears with the back of her hand. "That's how you helped Celia. You got to be a person while she was on vacation. Remember? When your brother kept chasing her?"

Raven groaned in exasperation. "How many times do I have to tell you that J.J. isn't a fairy? As for her brother—" His brows drew together. "Wait a minute. What brother?"

"She means Cord," J.J. supplied. "He played the troll in Jacq's third book."

That captured his interest. "You're kidding. Your sister made her own brother into a troll?"

"He's one of Jacq's most popular characters," she retorted defensively. "The children love him."

"He was very nice when he stopped being bad," River explained. She slipped from J.J.'s arms into her father's. "Please, Daddy," she whispered. "Please let Justice be my mommy for a little while. I'll be good for ever and ever if you say yes."

Raven closed his eyes. "Ah, sweetheart. It's not because you're bad," he assured softly, cradling her close. "You know that."

"But I want a mommy more than anything in the whole world." Her voice was muffled against the front of his shirt. "Even more than a puppy."

J.J. felt laughter fighting with tears. How could Raven resist such a plea? For that matter, how could she?

Raven swallowed convulsively. "I know you do. But isn't a dad good enough? It's always been the two of us. You and me. Best buds, remember?"

"Best buds," River repeated. "Forever and ever."

His jaw tightened. "You still want a mom, though, don't you?"

"Yes." The confession impacted like a blow. "I've been wishing and wishing as hard as I can."

Raven exhaled harshly, his face drawn into taut lines. "I...I didn't realize."

She peeked up at him. "I'll still love you best. I promise."

He chuckled, a gruff sound that fought a path from deep in his chest. "I know you will."

"So can I have her? For my mommy?"

Before he could say respond, the waitress returned. "Are you folks ready to order lunch?"

J.J. spared Raven the need to answer. "I think we need another minute," she said, tilting her head so she could look the woman in the eye instead of addressing her nylons and heels.

"Sure thing." The waitress shrugged as though it didn't matter, but her gaze remained sharply curious. "Holler when you're ready."

J.J. frowned, struck again by an eerie sense of familiarity. She'd never been to Denver before, and yet, she had the distinct impression she knew this woman. "Have we ever—"

"You're not from these parts, are you, Ms. Randell?" the waitress interrupted smoothly.

"No, I—" Perhaps it was the way the woman slipped in the question. Or perhaps it was the incongruity of the cheap mud brown dye job and ill-fitting uniform compared to her three-hundred-dollar pumps, silk stockings and manicured hands. More likely it was that hard-eyed stare. J.J. sighed. "No, I'm not from these parts, I'm not pregnant and since when did catering firms hire reporters?"

"Oops." The waitress chuckled. "Looks like my cover's been blown. Thanks for the update, Ms. Randell. Your name alone will be the bonus of a lifetime." Whipping off her cap and apron, she tossed them aside. "Enjoy your lunch, folks. Sorry I won't be able to fix it for you. But as Ms. Randell pointed out, I'm a reporter, not a waitress."

Raven released his breath in an exasperated sigh. "Ms. Lark. I can't believe I didn't recognize you."

The woman offered a pleased smile. "That *was* the idea. And just so you don't feel too bad…you were rather preoccupied."

"So I was." He gained his feet. "Seal exits on this floor, Gem," he ordered.

"AFFIRMATIVE. LOCK DOWN IN PROGRESS ON EXECUTIVE LEVEL."

"Lock down?" The reporter gave the doors exiting the dining area a quick look. A loud click issued from them as the lock snicked home. "Hey! You can't keep me here," she protested. "That's kidnapping or unlawful detainment or something."

"I'm arresting you for trespassing. It's called a citizen's arrest." Raven set his daughter on the floor before reaching down to assist J.J. to her feet. "Gem, alert security and the police."

"AFFIRMATIVE. CODE RED ALERT. CALL TO POLICE IN PROGRESS."

Ms. Lark moistened her lips and tried a friendly smile that didn't quite match her infuriated glare. "Look... I'm sure we can work out a deal."

"You're right. We can. The deal is that I'm going to have you locked up. With a little cooperation from some people I know, you'll be released tomorrow morning, by which time your information won't be worth quite as much." His slashing grin held even less amusement than the reporter's. "Thanks for visiting Sierra Consortium. It's a pleasure doing business with you."

"You won't get away with this!"

"Watch me." Cupping one hand around J.J.'s arm, he captured River with the other and headed for the door. "Gem, has security arrived?"

"AFFIRMATIVE."

"Unlock the door to the executive dining room." The minute the lock released, a half-dozen beefy security men filled the room. Raven murmured instructions to one of them. With a jerk of his head, he indicated that J.J. and River should precede him from the room. "We're leaving."

J.J. didn't argue. After seeing his ruthlessness in dealing with the reporter, she had no desire to be on the receiving end of another demonstration. "I'll need to get my coat and purse from your office."

"Make it fast. I want to get out of here before we pick up any more friends."

Leaving Raven issuing instructions to his secretary, J.J. returned to his office with River. While she gathered her possessions, the little girl collected her rag doll.

"Are you going to give me my wish now?" she asked.

"I don't know," J.J. confessed. "We didn't finish discussing it with your dad."

River lifted the doll to her shoulder and patted the cloth back. She peered over the yarn head, the expression in her huge blue eyes surprisingly serene. "You have to give me my wish even if you don't want to, you know."

J.J. paused, her brows drawing together. "Excuse me? I *have* to?" She didn't like the sound of that. She knew Raven adored his daughter, but surely he hadn't spoiled her so thoroughly that she automatically assumed she'd receive anything she wanted. "Why do I *have* to?"

"Because it's a wish," River explained matter-of-factly. "And Gem said birthday wishes always come true. So the wish will make you do it. That's how wishes work."

"The computer told you that?" J.J. couldn't conceal her astonishment. "Are you sure?"

"TIME IS OF THE ESSENCE. PLEASE VACATE PREMISES."

J.J.'s frown deepened. "Gem, did you tell River birthday wishes always come true?"

"AFFIRMATIVE."

"Why in the world would you do such a thing?" J.J. demanded in exasperation. "I can't believe someone programmed you for that."

"ASSUMPTION INCORRECT. INFORMATION PROVIDED BY DANI COLTER."

The name sounded vaguely familiar, but J.J. couldn't quite place it. "Who's Dani Colter?"

"MRS. DANI COLTER, FORMALLY SHERATON. CURRENTLY SPOUSAL UNIT OF NICK COLTER, OWNER OF SSI AND CREATOR OF GEM AND GEMINI UNITS."

Oh, right. J.J. recalled Raven mentioning Colter's name in connection with the computer. "But, Gem. What you've told River isn't accurate. Birthday wishes *don't* always come true."

Beside her, River caught her breath in a shocked gasp. "No, Justice. You can't have forgotten that, too. Birthday wishes always come true. Tell her, Gem!"

"CORRECT. WHEN APPROPRIATE CONDITIONS MET, WISH WILL BE GRANTED."

"Oh, for—" J.J. gave up arguing with the computer and stooped beside River. "Honey, it's wonderful to believe wishes can come true, but—"

"We did everything you're supposed to," River protested. "We did! Tell her, Gem."

"AFFIRMATIVE. NECESSARY PROCEDURE FOLLOWED EXACTLY."

"There *is* no procedure," J.J. retorted in exasperation.

"INCORRECT. ACCESSING PROCEDURE."

"You're a machine, Gem. How can you possibly—"

"WISH AVAILABLE ON PRECISE BIRTH ANNIVERSARY OF FEMALE OFFSPRING UNIT. DATE VERIFIED. REQUIRE DOUBLE-LAYERED TEN-INCH ROUND CONFECTIONERY FOOD ITEM WITH SUGAR COATING AND FLAMMABLE WAX INSERTS. PROVIDED."

"Gem, I know all about birthday cakes and candles—"

"SIX PINK INSERTS PLACED ON CONFECTION-

ERY FOOD ITEM. FLAMMABLE INSERT SUPPLIED FOR EACH BIRTHDAY. ONE EXTRANEOUS INSERT FOR BIRTHDAY-TO-GROW-ON. PROVIDED. FLAME APPLIED TO EACH INSERT. WISH MADE BEFORE FLAMES EXTINGUISHED. WISH KEPT SECRET FROM OTHER HUMANS. WISH SEQUENCE COMPLETED. ONE HUNDRED PERCENT COMPLIANCE AC-CORDED WISHING PRECEPTS.''

''That's lovely, Gem. But that doesn't mean that the wish will come true.''

''FACTS PROVIDED BY MRS. COLTER. MRS. COLTER HAS LEVEL ONE SECURITY CLEAR-ANCE.''

''That doesn't mean she knows what she's talking about,'' J.J. argued.

''ON BIRTH ANNIVERSARY OF MR. COLTER, MRS. COLTER ANNOUNCED THAT BIRTHDAY WISHES ALWAYS COME TRUE. MR. COLTER WISHED FOR SECOND OFFSPRING UNIT, WHICH ESTABLISHES ACCURACY OF STATEMENT.''

''That's not proof! That's basic human repro—'' J.J. darted a quick look in River's direction and amended what she'd been about to say. ''It's a coincidence.''

''ERROR NUMBER NINE-OH-NINE. ASSER-TIONS CONTRARY TO FACTS ON FILE.''

''That means you're wrong,'' River explained kindly. ''I do that error a lot.'' She slipped her hand into J.J.'s. ''Why don't you believe in birthday wishes? Don't fair-ies get them?''

J.J. sighed. ''I really don't know. Maybe I should call my sister and find out.''

''Okay.''

The door opened and Raven gestured to them. ''Let's move.''

Taking River by the hand, J.J. joined him in the reception area. "Do you know the sort of information Gem is feeding your daughter?"

Raven stabbed the call button for the elevator. "The computer has been specifically programmed to handle the level of information appropriate for a child of River's age and intellectual level."

"Is that a direct quote from SSI's sales manual?" she asked dryly. "Or from Gem?"

For a brief instance his guard dropped and a glorious smile flashed across his face. Good grief, but he was a stunning man when he chose to relax a little. "Caught me."

"Yeah, well I have news for you about that manual, not to mention your crazy computer—"

"ALL ELEVATORS CURRENTLY AT LOBBY LEVEL. WILL ARRIVE IN ONE MINUTE, THIRTY-THREE POINT TWO SECONDS," Gem interrupted. "LOCK DOWN STILL IN EFFECT ON EXECUTIVE LEVEL. CANCEL RED ALERT, MR. SIERRA?"

"Yes, Gem. And once the police are ready to leave you can cancel the lock down, as well."

"UNDERSTOOD."

Before J.J. could continue her conversation about his computer system, he asked, "So, what tipped you off?"

It took an instant to switch gears. "Oh, you mean with Ms. Lark?"

"Yes."

J.J. shrugged. "Designer nails, three-hundred-dollar shoes and silk stockings seemed wrong for a waitress. I suppose they're rather pricey for a reporter, too."

"If she worked for a reputable paper, you'd probably be right. But I suspect the information she sells keeps her well-heeled."

"Nicely put. I'd have noticed the inconsistency sooner except…" She shot River a pointed glance. "I was a bit distracted." Another concern occurred to her. "How much do you think Ms. Lark overheard?"

He shook his head. "I've been trying to remember what we were talking about when she was around. The wish, for sure. Our reaction to it, most likely. Who knows what else. I don't think security was recording at the time, or I'd have Gem play back the sequence."

"The computer records conversations?" J.J. asked, shocked at the idea.

He must have caught her adverse reaction. "I like to have a transcript for business purposes," he explained. "I always notify those present so it's not done without consent. But our lunch wasn't business."

Did Mathias do the same, she couldn't help but wonder? "I guess that means we have to try to remember what happened when."

"Between the two of us we should be able to figure it out."

"Well, for one thing, I suspect we blew the rumor about our engagement. We didn't react to River's request for a new mommy like your standard happily engaged couple. Nor would she need to wish for one if we were about to tie the knot."

"My fault, I'm afraid."

J.J. let that pass. His reasons for refusing to remarry were none of her business—no matter how curious she might be. She turned to face him. "Ms. Lark's going to be annoyed once she's released from jail."

"An understatement if I ever heard one. I think spitting mad is probably closer to it."

"Which means she'll want to get even."

"No doubt."

"If she figures out we're not engaged, I guarantee she'll put the worst possible spin on whatever she heard."

"Yes, Ms. Randell. I'm sure she will."

So they were back to formalities again. "Do you think you can keep her quiet for a full day?"

"Absolutely."

Which meant he had political clout. "That gives us time to put out our version first."

"I'm counting on it."

"Where are we going, Daddy?" River interrupted.

Raven's mouth tightened. "Someplace more private, where I can guarantee we won't be overheard. Then we'll finish talking about your wish."

The little girl crowed with excitement. "I'm gonna get my wish!"

"I didn't say that. I said we'd talk about it." The elevator arrived just then. "Direct access to parking garage level one, Gem. No stops," he ordered as they stepped into the car.

"AFFIRMATIVE, MR. SIERRA."

He leaned against the cloth-covered wall and folded his arms across his chest. "So go on, Ms. Randell. Precisely what version of our little fairy tale do you suggest I feed the papers?"

J.J. shrugged, wishing he'd volunteered more information about where he planned to take them, as well as what he wanted her to do about his daughter's latest wish. Unfortunately, with River listening to every word, she didn't dare ask. "It's your choice. But whichever version you decide on should cover as many angles as possible. That way any information Ms. Lark attempts to peddle tomorrow will sound like sour grapes."

"And you'll back up my story?"

She wished she could read his thoughts, understand precisely what he was asking. But they remained shrouded. The man had had a lot of practice at maintaining an impenetrable facade. Too much practice. "Do I have a choice?"

"No."

"Then why ask?"

The elevator car slowed to a stop and the doors parted, revealing a parking garage. Crossing to a black Mercedes, he opened the door to the back seat and waited while River scrambled in. "Fasten your seat belt," he instructed before closing the door.

"I assume you'll announce the engagement," J.J. said, starting for the car.

"That's one option."

"What's the other?"

"I can tell the press the truth."

J.J. stopped in her tracks. Oh, no! She caught his arm, staring at him in alarm. He tensed beneath her touch, but she scarcely noticed. "I'd rather you didn't reveal Mathias's part in all this."

"Protecting your dear brother-in-law?"

She saw no point in denying it. "Yes. If people find out he routinely grants Christmas wishes, he'll be inundated with requests. And when he's unable to fulfill all of them, he'll be vilified. After what's happened with River, you should be able to sympathize with that."

It was his turn to grasp her arm, wrapping powerful fingers around her wrist. He planted his other hand at the base of her spine and pulled her against him. His tension instantly communicated itself to her. Before she could do more than gasp a quick protest, he lowered his head so his mouth brushed her cheek.

"Sympathize, Ms. Randell? With Mathias Blackstone? I don't think so."

# CHAPTER FIVE

The prince crept quietly through the underbrush, his sword drawn. The odor of dragon clung strongly to the ferns and trees and bushes—the few that hadn't been scorched by the hot breath of the ferocious beast.

The prince had been coming to the forest for years, searching...always searching for the great dragon, Nemesis. This was the closest he'd ever come to finding the creature's secret lair. He smiled in triumph. Finally he had the chance to succeed at his goal, a goal he'd committed his life to achieving—the death of the dragon who'd killed his family.

Page 17, *The Great Dragon Hunt,*
by Jack Rabbitt

"DON'T!" J.J. tried to pull free, but Raven refused to release her, constraining her with frightening ease.

"Be quiet and listen," he ordered.

To an outsider they undoubtedly looked like a loving couple sharing an intimate embrace. But she knew differently. He held her this close to prevent River from overhearing, his comments for her ears alone.

He shifted his stance ever so slightly and J.J. felt every ripple and surge of the muscles ridging his shoulders and arms. To her horror, her response hit hard, an unexpected rush of sheer feminine need. *Not now, please not now,* she silently begged. It was a fruitless plea. Her fingers itched to explore, to unbutton his shirt and caress the warm flesh beneath. To rip his tie from its moorings and press her lips to the bronzed hollow at the base of his neck. To lift her face to his and take his mouth in a fierce, endless kiss, one that would mark him as hers—and hers alone.

His warm breath caressed her heated cheeks, playing across the tips of her lashes and the fullness of her mouth. But that didn't bother her nearly as much as the way their hips locked together, fitting in perfect opposition. His thighs were taut against hers, causing a liquid warmth to quicken, running riot through every inch of her. She burned with it—the need to find completion with this man. She stirred in helpless agony, the air shuddering from her lungs.

"Say what you have to and let me go." *Please let go!* Before she gave into the desire begging to be tasted. Before she lost what little self-control she still retained and took what she wanted most.

"Pay attention, fairy lady. I'm only going to say this once."

*Thank heavens!* She bit back the words before they could escape, knowing they would only incite him—something he clearly didn't need. "Go ahead and get it over with."

"Don't you dare ask me to sympathize with Blackstone. He spun this particular ball into play, which means he'll just have to live with the consequences of his action.''

She braved his gaze, praying her response didn't show in her eyes. Could he see? Could he tell how profoundly he affected her? "What about River? Will she have to live with the consequences, too?"

His eyes were so dark, so impassioned. She felt the tension building across his chest, saw it in the determined set of his jaw. For an instant his hand tightened on her wrist. But before she could even register the impact, he loosened his hold and his touch gentled. Muted power. Diamond-hard tenderness. A warrior with honor, wise enough to guard against his own vulnerability with as much vigilance as he guarded those beneath his protection.

"I won't allow my daughter to be hurt by him."

"Be careful that you aren't so intent on getting even with Mathias that you don't hurt her yourself," she warned.

It was a direct hit. Hot color swept along the edges of his cheekbones and she could practically hear the growl of fury rumbling through his chest. "We wouldn't be in this situation if it weren't for him," Raven informed her harshly.

"It was a wish," she whispered. "Just a wish."

"One he never should have offered." Coldness encased his anger. "You've given me the perfect weapon for payback. Blackstone doesn't want anyone to know about his antics? Tough. The instant I'm certain River won't be harmed by his 'generosity,' he's going down. Hard."

With that he released her and stalked to the Mercedes. He opened the front passenger door. "Let's go. We don't have a lot of time."

She fought for composure, to conceal how badly he'd upset her. It wasn't just what he'd said, but her reaction to him physically, as well. His body had imprinted on hers like a physical brand. That had been disastrous enough. But it was how he'd affected her emotionally that distressed her most of all. She'd always been so careful to protect herself. So careful to hold men at a distance, to avoid losing control. And in one easy move, Raven Sierra had stripped her of that ability.

Taking a deep breath, she crossed to the car and slid inside. The entire way to her hotel, she didn't say a word. Once there, she packed the few extra garments and toiletries she'd purchased that morning and checked out. Since Raven and his daughter both accompanied her to the room, she didn't try and phone Mathias again. Nor were there any messages waiting. That in particular shook her. Apparently she'd been left to her own devices, which meant remaining at the mercy of a man intent on protecting his child from harm—harm in the form of a woman bearing wishes.

It put her in a very precarious position.

Within the hour they'd picked up the lunch they'd missed and were headed away from the city, toward the mountains. Unable to bear the silence any longer, she finally asked, "So, where are we going?"

"As I told River, somewhere private."

Men! "Could you be more specific?"

"I recently completed construction on a cabin. We'll talk there."

"We're going to the mountains?" River questioned excitedly.

A cabin in the mountains? J.J. settled against the leather seat, relaxing slightly. That sounded interesting. She'd enjoy spending an afternoon seeing something of the surrounding area before catching her flight back to Seattle. "Great."

Raven looked in the rearview mirror. "River, why

don't you close your eyes, sweetheart. We should be there by the time you wake up.''

"I don't want to take a nap,'' she instantly protested.

"River.''

"Will you let me stay up late if I take a nap?''

"River.''

"Just until it's dark so I can see the moon.''

J.J. stiffened. "Er…the moon back in Denver, right?'' she interrupted in alarm.

Raven shot her an amused look. "Last time I checked they were both the same one.'' He glanced in the rear-view mirror again, addressing his daughter. "If the moon doesn't come up too late, that's fine.''

"Wait a minute—''

"That's not a yes,'' he added. "That's a maybe.''

"A maybe's close to a yes, right?'' River demanded.

"Close. But not there, yet. Now go on to sleep.''

"Okay.''

"No! Not okay,'' J.J. protested, swiveling in her seat to face Raven. "I thought you said we were going to the cabin to talk.''

"We are.'' He'd set his jaw in a stubborn slant, a posture she'd come to recognize as a bad sign. It meant she didn't have a hope of winning the coming argument. "It's just that our conversation might take a few days.''

She fought to speak around the tightness gripping her chest. No. No way. She wouldn't allow him to bend her to his will as her father had always done. "I don't have a few days. I have a plane to catch tonight.''

Raven shrugged. "I'm afraid you're going to miss it. I suggest you reschedule. You can ask Gem to make new reservations when we get to the cabin.''

It was becoming more difficult to breathe. "I want to go back to Denver. Right *now*.''

Something in J.J.'s expression warned that she was dead serious. Raven spared a quick look at his daughter.

The last two days had clearly taken their toll. She'd already fallen asleep, curled in a dainty ball despite the restriction of the seat belt. Carefully, he pulled off onto a rough dirt side road.

"Okay, Ms. Randell. Let's talk."

Without a word, she thrust open the door and scrambled from the car. A light autumn breeze caught her hair, tossing it around her shoulders like a matador's cape. Aspen framed her, the white bark and golden leaves a sharp foil against her vibrant coloring. She presented him with her back, her arms wrapped around her waist. He reached into the car and removed her coat. Crossing to her side, he dropped it around her shoulders, enclosing her in warmth.

"Will River be okay in the car alone?" she asked. She didn't turn around, but he noticed she snuggled deeper into the soft woolen folds.

"She's out cold. She won't overhear anything we say and we're three steps from the car if she needs us."

J.J. inclined her head. "Okay. So, let's talk. In case I haven't made myself clear, I want to return to Denver. Now, please."

How rigid she sounded, with just the merest thread of anxiety underscoring her words. It was that anxiety that got to him. "I owe you an apology," Raven said with a rough sigh. "I should have asked first before dragging you out here."

That did bring her around. "You're darned right you should have. No one makes decisions for me. No one."

"I'll remember in future," he replied evenly. "But that doesn't change the situation. We have to settle our problem with River's wish. And we're not going to do it back in Denver."

A streak of vibrant red marked her cheeks and an angry sparkle darkened her honey brown eyes. For the first time she truly looked like the fairy River adored so fiercely. And for the first time he realized the difference between the image Jack Rabbitt had created and the actual woman. Justice was free to live life to the fullest—free to express her emotions, naked physically as well as spiritually. But not J.J. She remained fully shrouded, tiptoeing through life with great care, as though the world were made of eggshells and one false step would send her plummeting into a frightening void.

"You don't like losing control, do you?" he observed.

"Losing it?" She laughed, the sound tinged with a hint of irony. "Considering how rarely I've ever been in control, I'm not sure it's possible for me to lose it."

"Interesting." Raven's regard intensified. Now what—or more likely *who*—had managed to steal this woman's innate inner power? "And why are you so rarely the one in control?" he asked.

She instantly turned wary, quick to rebuild her defenses, cloaking herself in frost and icicles. It magnified his curiosity, making him wonder what would happen if she ever fully cut loose. "I don't like having my decisions made for me," she informed him tightly. "You had no business taking me to your cabin without discussing it first."

"You're right. That's why we're standing here. So we can discuss it now." He approached, fascinated by the way she held her ground when he could see how badly she wanted to retreat. Brave woman. "I have a brandnew, fully stocked cabin not far from Denver. It's isolated and, best of all, the reporters haven't discovered it yet, which means we can settle our problems in private. Will you come?"

"For how long?"

He shrugged. "For as long as it takes. A day. Two."

"A week?"

"If it becomes necessary."

Alarm broke across her expression. "You know that's

not possible. I only came to Denver for a few hours—a day tops. I didn't even bring spare clothes with me. I spent the morning shopping for what little I do have."

"I can make arrangements for anything you need."

Her lips compressed. "I have to get back to work."

"Really?" He lifted an eyebrow, his voice ever so gently mocking. "I thought you were at work. Isn't giving River her wish your current assignment?"

"Yes, but—"

Unable to resist, he stepped closer. At what point would he break through to the woman frozen beneath the protective ice? What would it take for J.J. to become Justice? If this really were a fairy tale, a kiss would be the solution. Too bad she didn't look like a woman waiting to be awakened by love's first kiss. He forced himself to be honest. Brutally honest. He had no love to give, even if she were open to receiving it. Though it might be interesting to see the transition in both of them if he gave it a try.

"It should have only taken a day," J.J. was explaining—more to herself, he suspected, than to him. "I couldn't even go home and pack. The memo said I had to leave immediately and—"

"You came. You promised River a wish. And now you want to leave without fulfilling it. Nice."

He'd hit his mark, as he'd intended. She didn't say anything for a long moment. Instead she turned and gazed out at the surrounding landscape as though it held the answers she sought. The wind swept past, pausing only long enough for them to sample its chilly bite before rushing off to summon a rainbow-hued whirlwind from the drifts of fallen leaves.

J.J. withdrew deeper into the soft folds of her coat. She'd raised the collar so the black lamb's wool kissed her pale jawline, creating a sharp contrast of black on white, textured on smooth. In that instant, she didn't seem quite real anymore, more like a bittersweet illusion that momentarily displaced the harshness of reality.

"She wants a mother," J.J. murmured at last and the illusion vanished, just as all fantasies did. "Did you realize she'd made it her birthday wish?"

"Not at the time." He couldn't manage more than that. He'd give his daughter the earth, if he could, even throw in the sun and stars as an afterthought. But to provide her with a mother—one possibly like Maise… He couldn't bring himself to do it. Anything but that.

"What happened to her mother?" So soft. So gently asked.

"She died."

"I'm sorry." She wasn't going to let it drop, he could tell. Sure enough, she turned slightly, slanting those exotic honeyed eyes in his direction. "Does River remember her?"

"Maise died when River was only a few weeks old." Compassion dawned in J.J.'s expression and he wanted to wipe it out even as he wanted to drown in it. It was his turn to withdraw, to push temptation to a safe distance. "If you lived here, you'd have read about it in the papers. Or Ms. Lark could have filled you in, if only you'd known to ask."

The collar brushed her jaw again. Black on white, textured on smooth. Sweet fantasy displacing harsh reality. His hands clenched. It had been so damned long. Too damned long. What a shame he no longer believed in fantasies.

"I don't think I'd have liked Ms. Lark's version," J.J. murmured. "She doesn't strike me as the most empathetic woman in the world."

"Let's just say Ms. Lark has a lurid imagination. Her version was rather damning." He shrugged it off. "It isn't important."

But, apparently, he'd said too much. That, or else he'd

underestimated J.J.'s intuitive powers. Comprehension slipped to the surface, shadowing her eyes. "Ms. Lark blamed you for Maise's death, didn't she?"

"Good guess." Time to put the delectable Ms. Randell in her place—a place as far from him as possible. "It made for amusing reading, all about how my wife and I were on the verge of divorce. How relieved I was when Maise died because I received full custody of my daughter without a nasty courtroom battle."

"Oh, no!"

He smiled, actually amused by her appalled reaction. "Haven't you guessed, sweetheart? According to the papers, I drove my wife to her death. Two short weeks after the birth of our daughter, I forced Maise from the house during a thunderstorm wearing only a thin nightgown. She died of pneumonia six days later. It's common knowledge. The papers reported the entire incident. Since then I've been Mr. Untouchable. No woman touches me. And I touch no woman." His smile grew, deliberately sharp and biting. "Until now."

J.J. tilted her head to one side, her hair a black satin waterfall over the front of her coat. Temptation beckoned again, urging him to fist his hand around that soft slide of silk. To drag it to his mouth, then drag her to his mouth. To consume her as if she were a long-awaited feast.

"Is that what I should believe, too?" she asked with impressive calm. "Or is that what you're *hoping* I'll believe?"

"Does it matter?"

"I suspect it does."

He managed a laugh. "You're wrong. It doesn't matter in the least." Deliberately he turned his too-observant fairy lady in a new direction. "Shall we move this conversation along? After all, you're not here to grant *my* wish, are you, Ms. Randell?"

"No."

Was that a hint of regret he heard? He hardened himself against the possibility. "I didn't think so. Continuing this particular line of discussion is pointless." He jammed his hands into his pockets. "I suggest we focus on River and find a way to accomplish her wish with the least amount of hassle, in the least amount of time. And I suggest we decide on a story to release to the newspapers."

"Fine with me. Let's start with River. She wants a mother, you know."

"She wants *you*."

Her breath escaped in an exasperated sigh. "So what do we do? If I agree to play the part of her mother during your vacation, won't it cause even more harm when her wish finally comes to an end?"

"Possibly. Or perhaps she'll realize that the fantasy isn't as much fun as she'd hoped."

He could see her puzzling over his words, gradually putting the correct construction on them. "You think once I've been around her for a while she'll decide that J.J., the person, isn't as fun as Justice, the fairy?"

"Are you?"

"No," she confessed. "Justice is my sister's fantasy, not mine."

"It's also River's."

She turned sharply away, but not before he saw the desolation that tainted her expression. "Too bad Jacq isn't still available," she said with a lightness that didn't quite ring true. "She'd have been the perfect mother. She's imaginative, fun, outgoing, adores children. And they adore her."

Interesting. He'd have said the same about J.J. "You don't share those qualities?" he asked, curious to see how she'd respond.

"I'm the practical one of the family."

He laughed. "Yeah, right."

She threw a surprised look over her shoulder. "You don't believe me?"

"In a word...no. I've looked into the eyes of too many dreamers not to recognize one when she shows up and offers me a handful of stardust and moonbeams."

She swung fully around. "Obviously you haven't looked closely enough. I'm the least imaginative person you'll ever meet. I'm so grounded in reality, I have roots."

He regarded her with genuine amusement. "Keep telling yourself that, sweetheart, and maybe it'll come true." Then he added pointedly, "When you're not running around the countryside fulfilling ridiculous wishes, that is."

He'd succeeded in irritating her again. The fairy buried deep inside quivered to life, fighting for release.

"It's apparent you've made up your mind about me," she retorted. "Which probably means your idea will work just fine. River isn't the only one in for a shock. You're in for one, too. Despite what you think, I'm not Justice. In fact, I'm nothing like her. I'm an ordinary, practical woman. Boringly normal," she stressed.

Yeah, right. No one would ever call J.J. Randell ordinary, let alone "boringly normal." She might hide behind those labels, but they weren't even close to accurate. She was shades of black on shades of white, deeply textured on icy smooth, a winged fantasy trying to pass for grounded reality.

And he wanted her.

He forced himself to focus, a feat becoming more and more difficult with each passing moment. "I assume that means you agree to River's alternate wish," he said.

His comment brought her up short and he almost laughed out loud at her expression. So much for playing the part of Ms. Practical. She couldn't even stay connected to reality long enough to realize what she'd committed herself to.

"I...I guess I have," she conceded. "What about the reporter? We were going to discuss how to handle that problem, too."

"I want to release a statement announcing our engagement. Considering what Ms. Lark overheard, it's the very least we need to do."

She nodded reluctantly. "Time for damage control."

"Past time."

"Will announcing our engagement be enough to spike her guns?"

"No. That's why I'm going to embellish a little." He waited, expecting her to ask for details. When she didn't, he let it go. She'd find out soon enough. No sense in upsetting her any further today. "Questions?" he prompted.

"When is this vacation to start?"

"Apparently it already has."

She frowned. "And how long will it last?"

"A week. No longer than ten days."

"I'll have to check with Mathias and make sure he can spare me that long."

His amusement faded at the reminder. If this didn't work out the way he hoped, Blackstone would pay. No one—*no one*—hurt his daughter and got away with it. "Since this was his brilliant idea, he'll have to find a way to spare you."

"I don't think he anticipated River's wish."

"Then he shouldn't have gotten involved." His words were harsher than he'd planned and he instantly regretted how deeply they bit. Had she any idea how revealing her eyes could be, how the brown deepened to umber whenever he upset her? He doubted it. Nor would she like it if she knew. "Any other problems or concerns? I'd like to get a move on."

"My...my clothes."

It cost her a lot to ask. The last thing he wanted was for her to sacrifice her pride over something so minor. "There's a small town not far from the cabin," he assured easily. "We can shop there. Can you hold out until tomorrow?"

"Sure."

He could tell she desperately wanted to come up with some more objections. "Then we have a deal?" he asked before she could think of any. "You'll play the part of River's mother for the length of our vacation. Do whatever she asks—"

"Within reason," J.J. hastened to interrupt.

"Within reason. And you'll try your best to disillusion her."

"Wait a minute. I never agreed—"

"All I'm asking is that you be yourself," he explained impatiently. "You claim to be practical. Make sure you are. Don't feed into her fantasies if you can help it. She's susceptible enough without your encouraging her."

"I'll be myself. I can't promise more than that."

Be herself. That's what he was afraid of. She might buy into all that bull about being unimaginative and practical, but it wouldn't last. A fairy hid deep within her, struggling for freedom. He'd already seen it battle its way to the surface a time or two. Once that wondrous creature found a way to permanently escape, practicality would be out the window.

Just like Maise.

"Is there anything else we need to discuss?" she questioned impatiently.

"Not that I can think of."

"Fine. Then let's go."

She started for the car and he suddenly recalled he hadn't warned her about the sleeping accommodations. "Ms. Randell?"

"Yes?"

She turned, her hair seized by a rogue gust of wind. The long, dark strands billowed around her in an untamed torrent, just as it had when she'd ridden naked on the back of a butterfly. The illusion winked into existence again and he didn't resist. Couldn't resist. He closed in on her, filling his hands with her hair. He marveled briefly at its softness, surprised to discover it was as silken-fine as he'd imagined. Pillowing it against the soft curve of her cheeks, he gathered her in.

"I've been waiting to taste you since the first time you walked through my door," he told her roughly.

"No—"

But whether she was denying his statement or her own yearnings, he wasn't certain. He lowered his head and her resistance ebbed, slipping from her like evening surrendering to the night. Gently he stole a kiss, his mouth brushing hers in a whisper-soft caress. It was undeniably a first sampling, one filled as much with curiosity as it was with sharp, desperate need. Unable to resist, he returned for another. And then another, each kiss learning more, sharing more. Each one growing deeper and more urgent than the last. It wasn't enough. Not nearly enough.

"Open for me," he murmured. "Let me in."

"A dangerous request," she whispered, her eyes falling shut. "Very dangerous."

"A practical woman would stop me. A practical woman would keep her lips closed nice and tight." He brushed her mouth once more. Teasing. Tempting. Seducing. "Are you, fairy lady? Are you a practical woman?"

Her moan trembled in the air between them. "Yes, I am. I'm the most practical woman you'll ever meet." And then she thrust her hands deep into his hair, tugging him downward.

Her lips were moist and eager, sliding over his in joyous union. She opened to him and he dipped swiftly inward, groaning at her lush taste, finding the unique flavor sweeter than any he'd ever known. She was delicious warmth and wild passion, burning desire and sweet heat. And if there'd been a bed anywhere within reach, he'd have had her in it, stripped as naked as a fairy riding a butterfly.

Her hair drifted from his hands in an ebony cascade as he sought the smooth silk of her skin, his thumbs stroking the high sweep of her cheekbones. He wanted more of her. He wanted all of her. He pulled her close, impatient with the layers of wool barring his path.

"Why are you wearing so many damned clothes?" he demanded.

She chuckled, the sound shuddering straight through him. "It's cold outside."

"Bull. It's hotter than Hades." Her sweater provided a momentary barrier until he found where it joined her skirt. "You sure as hell don't need this," he said, sweeping upward beneath the pullover.

She released a startled gasp and he caught it in his mouth, drinking it in. Where earlier he'd filled his hands with her hair, now something infinitely softer and more feminine filled them. He wished he could strip away her sweater, taste what he could only touch. But that wasn't possible. At least, not here. Not when she couldn't fully appreciate the experience. The tips of her breasts surged against his palms, turgid buds that betrayed her passion.

"You feel it, too, don't you?" he asked. He rocked her into the cradle of his hips so she'd know she wasn't alone in her reaction. So she'd know that he, too, burned with an unrelenting need.

J.J. buried her face in the crook of his shoulder. "This shouldn't be happening."

"Oh, no? It can't come as a surprise. Hell, we've been

eyeing each other ever since you arrived. I'm just amazed I had the strength of will to walk away last night.''

She laughed, the sound filled with despair. ''You don't understand. I'm not like this. I've never kissed a man on the side of the road. Not someone I've only known for a day. And I certainly never allowed him to…to…''

''To do this…?'' Ever so gently, he palmed her breasts, stroking the satiny skin with callused fingertips.

A shiver rippled through her and her breath hitched in her throat. ''Yes, that.''

''You want me to stop?''

''It would be the smart thing to do.''

Raven glanced at her curiously. It wouldn't appear that the smart thing held much appeal. She lifted her gaze to his and what he read there brought a regretful smile to his lips. ''Another time, perhaps,'' he murmured.

''I'm playing the part of River's mother, remember?'' Her breath came in sweet little puffs, swift and warm and urgent. ''Not the part of your wife.''

He grinned. ''Maybe I should have River amend that wish.''

She dragged free of his arms, her movements decisive. ''Not a chance,'' she retorted. But her lips trembled with desperate need and her eyes burned incandescent with unsated hunger. For a split second, she swayed, bending once again toward temptation. At the last possible instant, she caught herself. And turning, she strode toward the car.

He didn't try to stop her. *Face it, Sierra.* She was an enchantment too bewitching to resist. A brilliant fantasy that had no business invading his dark reality. He knew all about fantasies. They were rainbows that drew the unwary on impossible quests, melting into nothing the instant they were captured. They were exquisite dreams that slipped away with dawn's first light, stealing even the memory of their own beauty. They were untouchable and unwanted.

He watched silently as she vanished into the passenger seat.

Black on white.

Textured on smooth.

The bittersweet illusion of fantasy, fading beneath the harsh, revealing light of reality.

# CHAPTER SIX

Justice snuggled deep into the vivid red pocket of a tulip. A feathery stamen tickled her cheek, leaving behind a streak of yellow pollen. She brushed it away, but more rained down on her head, powdering her long black hair with gold dust. The wind tossed the top-heavy flower, laughing at her, teasing her as she bobbed helplessly back and forth.

"You know I can't catch you," she called to the wind. With a sigh, she rolled onto her back and slipped deeper into the mouth of the tulip, her feet dangling over the pouty outer lips. For that was the next "gift" required by Fausta. Somehow she was to capture wind, fire, water and earth and add the four elements to her silken bag. But how in all of Fairy was she to accomplish such an impossibility?

Page 22, *The Great Dragon Hunt*
by Jack Rabbitt

To J.J.'s relief, River woke shortly after they returned to the car. She provided an instant distraction, something J.J. sorely needed.

"Daddy, when are we going to get there?"

"Not for a while."

Why had Raven kissed her? She risked a quick glance in his direction and found him concentrating on the road. And why had she responded so ardently? It had been a dangerous slip on her part. She might find him attractive, but she had to exhibit more self-control. Intimacy equaled danger. She couldn't forget that. She *wouldn't* forget that.

"You said we'd be there when I woke up," River complained.

"Sorry, sweetheart. We were delayed."

J.J. frowned. She didn't understand how he could slip beneath her guard with such ease. She'd have thought two such wary individuals wouldn't have had any difficulty holding each other at a distance. They were both experienced enough at the art. Her gaze slid to his profile again. Very experienced. Guarded. Private. Defenses at full alert. And yet...

"What does delayed mean, Gem?" River demanded.

"Gem's not hooked up to the car, remember?"

"No, I forgot."

"Well, you can talk to the computer when we get to the cabin."

And yet, they'd tumbled into each other's arms as though desperate for human contact. J.J. caught her lower lip between her teeth. Perhaps that explained it. Perhaps it had been so long since they'd allowed themselves to touch and be touched that the need had grown to intolerable levels. Her mouth curved downward. Or perhaps she'd worked PR for so long she'd gotten used to coating the truth with a more palatable layer of BS.

Because the truth was... She wanted Raven every bit

as much as he wanted her. If they'd been anywhere other than in the open where someone could have stumbled across them, he'd have driven that point home. And she wouldn't have lifted a single finger to stop him.

"Daddy, call Gem on the telephone and ask what delayed means," River requested.

"I don't need to ask the computer. Delayed means we've been slowed down so it's going to take longer to get there than I told you."

J.J. closed her eyes. *Okay, sweetie. Time to face facts.* For some inexplicable reason, her libido went into overdrive every time she came within shouting distance of Raven. Even now she could feel the desire simmering between them as if it were a hot, focused current, arching and crackling the closer they came. Maybe now that she'd acknowledged it, she'd be able to control it.

She almost laughed out loud. Oh, sure. How difficult could it be? All she needed to do was shore up a few sagging defenses, keep her hands off Mr. Raven Sierra, make sure the man kept his hands off her—and pray this wish didn't delay her return to Seattle for much longer.

"Oh, rats," River grumbled. "I don't like being delayed."

Raven turned his head and looked at J.J. Just one quick glance. But it warned that he knew precisely what she'd been thinking. "I doubt we'll be delayed for much longer," he murmured. "At least, I won't."

And with that single, all-too-telling comment, her defenses fell. Hard.

"This is your cabin?" J.J. asked dryly, an interminable hour later. She stepped out onto the gravel driveway and looked around.

Raven cut the engine of the car and thrust open his door. "This is it."

"You have a talent for understatement."

His "cabin" was a huge stone, wood and glass structure that had somehow been slipped in among the surrounding aspen and pines. Perched on a steep mountainside, it overlooked a gorgeous meadow. A stream gurgled down the hill nearby, tripping musically over rocks and stones and around trees and bushes before meandering through the grassy area below.

He shrugged. "I wanted privacy."

"I think you succeeded."

The inside was equally impressive. J.J. stood in the entranceway, admiring the open floor plan and the simplicity of the decor. To her left she could see a huge living area, and a stone fireplace occupied one entire wall. To her right, she caught a glimpse of a kitchen and casual dining area.

"My bedroom's upstairs," River said, grabbing hold of J.J.'s hand. "It's right next to Daddy's. Do you wanna see it?"

"I'd love to."

The bedrooms were situated at the top of a short staircase between the living room and kitchen. River proudly showed off her own room before allowing J.J. to peek into Raven's. That's when it struck her.

"Wait a minute." She turned, practically tumbling into Raven's arms. Sneaky devil. "Where am I supposed to sleep?"

"Didn't I mention?" His attempt at an innocent look must have been the same one Hades gave Persephone—just before he fed his captive the pomegranate seeds that condemned her to spending four months of every year in the Underworld. "The cabin only has two bedrooms. One for our daughter…and one for us."

"Why can't I use the dirt outside?" River whispered worriedly, snuggling deeper beneath the covers.

"INSTRUCTIONS ARE SPECIFIC. GIFT MUST BE

EARTH THAT CONTAINS A SPECIAL QUALITY. EXTERIOR DIRT DOES NOT HAVE ANY SPECIAL QUALITIES. YOU ARE REQUIRED TO CONSIDER A SECONDARY OPTION.''

"Don't use so many big words," River scolded. "I don't understand."

"PICK DIRT THAT IS SPECIAL."

"Oh." She rolled over onto her tummy and felt beneath the pillow, reassured when her fingers touched the cover of her Jack Rabbitt book. Gently she traced the outline of the great dragon, Nemesis. "Where do I get special dirt?''

A momentary silence greeted her question. "INSUFFICIENT INFORMATION FOR RESPONSE."

"Huh?"

"ANSWER UNAVAILABLE."

"You don't know, do you?"

"AFFIRMATIVE."

"Do all the gifts have to be special?"

"AFFIRMATIVE."

"Oh." River mulled that over before another question occurred to her. "Do I have to get wind first?"

"ONE MOMENT. ACCESSING." A series of beeps issued from nearby speakers, then Gem said, "SEQUENCE NOT GIVEN. NINETY-EIGHT PERCENT PROBABILITY THAT ORDER IS UNIMPORTANT TO FINAL OUTCOME. INSTRUCTIONS REQUIRE GIFTS MUST BE OBTAINED, PLACED IN SILK BAG AND THANKS GIVEN. NO OTHER PARAMETERS SET."

"Gem!"

"PICK ONE GIFT. PLACE IN BAG. SAY THANK YOU. ERROR CAUSES FAILURE."

"I did that already. And Daddy said if he caught me sneaking outside again he'd punish me."

"STEALTH IS NECESSARY TO AVOID DETECTION."

"Huh?"

"YOU MUST BE QUIET WHEN GOING OUTSIDE."

"I know *that*. I'll be more careful next time." She yawned, burrowing deeper into the warmth of her bed. "So if I get some fire tomorrow and put it in my purse, it'll work?"

"WARNING. PLACING FLAME IN SILK PURSE MAY RESULT IN DANGEROUS SITUATION."

"I'm not gonna burn up my purse," River scoffed. "This is a *special* fire. Just like you said it should be."

"UNDERSTOOD."

"Gem?"

"PROCEED."

"Will this work?"

"CURRENT PROBABILITY TWENTY-TWO POINT SEVEN PERCENT CHANCE OF SUCCESS."

"Is that good?"

"NEGATIVE."

River clutched her rag doll to her chest. "Does that mean it won't work?" She waited anxiously for the response.

"INFORMATION UNAVAILABLE," Gem replied. And then in a surprisingly soft voice the computer added, "BIRTHDAY WISHES ALWAYS COME TRUE."

Sleep beckoned. "Justice will be my mommy?" she managed to ask.

"BIRTHDAY WISHES ALWAYS COME TRUE," Gem repeated. "FAILURE UNACCEPTABLE."

"Did you get her to bed?" J.J. asked.

"Yes."

The word shattered the darkened hallway, harsh, bitten-off and tarnished with bleak memories. But he couldn't help it. Finding River on the deck, standing cold and barefoot in her thin little nightie, had brought the horror of that long-ago night crashing in on him.

"Did she say what she was doing outside this late?"

"She said something about the moon and the stars and saying thank-you. Whatever the hell that means."

He thrust a hand through his hair. For the thousandth time he assured himself that River wouldn't be harmed from a brief outing on such a clear, if chilly, evening. She wasn't already sick with bronchitis as Maise had been and she hadn't gotten wet. He closed his eyes. River was safe. Perfectly safe.

But she reminded him of his wife, a fact which flat-out terrified him. Maise with her corn-ripe hair and glorious silver-blue eyes, the fever giving her cheeks a rosy flush. Maise standing drenched beneath an icy downpour, enacting some crazy New Age, spiritualistic mumbo-jumbo ritual. Giving thanks for the safe birth of their daughter, she'd said between hacking coughs.

Giving thanks. Yeah, right. Foolish. Stupid. Idiotic. Pointless.

Fatal.

Raven set his jaw. Fantasies had killed his wife, but they sure as hell weren't going to harm his daughter. He'd done everything within his powers to eradicate their influence in her life—with one notable exception: *Jack Rabbitt*. Clearly that single indulgence had been a dangerous mistake, one he intended to correct at his earliest convenience.

He shifted away from the closed door of his daughter's bedroom and headed for the steps leading downstairs. J.J. trailed him. "Did you tell her that I'd agreed to fulfill her wish? Could that be it?"

"No. I decided to wait until morning so she wouldn't get too excited at bedtime." He frowned. "Something else has set her off. I just don't know what, yet." He stalked into the kitchen and snatched a canister of coffee from the countertop. "Want some?"

"Thanks. I'd appreciate it."

Good. Let her stay. He wanted her nearby. He wanted to curse her for coming into their lives, even as he wanted to scoop her up in his arms and love her until dawn splintered the horizon. He balked at the knowledge, at the solace she could provide. Instead he embraced the richness of his anger, embraced the storm swirling relentlessly closer.

"It's this damn wish business. It's feeding into her fantasies." He dumped several scoops of ground beans into a filter, his movements a picture of muted violence. "She probably thinks anything's possible now."

"I...I'm sorry." So soft. So sweet. A gentle breeze attempting to calm a raging tempest. "I had no idea that River would make the wish she did."

"Blackstone knew." And the bastard would pay for his interference.

"You can't be sure of that. He probably thought he was doing you a favor."

Ah. Much better. She'd decided to buffet the storm instead of redirect it. He turned, his warning smile a flash of white in the darkness of his face. "A favor?" He gave her a taste of the elemental forces driving him, allowing a hint of temper to sweep into his voice. "By presuming to give my daughter a wish without asking me first?"

"Under other circumstances—"

"No!" The vortex drew ever closer, pulling, tugging, driving. "Under *these* circumstances. It's a wish you can never fulfill. A wish that, ultimately, will bring my daughter nothing but misery."

Her anger rose to match his. He could see it in those expressive brown eyes. Feel it reach out for him. And he reveled in it, needing the emotional turbulence to cleanse him of past guilt.

She planted her hands on her hips and faced him down. Heaven help him, but she was beautiful. Her cheeks blossomed as vividly as winter roses against a pallet of ebony hair. Her eyes burned like hot, sweet honey, and her mouth glistened damply, waiting to be plundered again. Only the butcher block in the center of the kitchen separated them—a barrier he could vault in two seconds flat. What would she do if he came over it after her? Would she resist…or submit? Or would she turn the aggressor, thrusting her hands into his hair and demanding he kiss her again? The memory of their earlier encounter shuddered through him.

"If you don't think I can fulfill River's wish, then why didn't you drop me off at the airport instead of bringing me here?" she asked.

Because he couldn't let her go. Because some dangerous part of him wanted a fairy lady in his life every bit as much as his daughter. And that knowledge infuriated him. "Because River believes in you. She's obsessed with this fantasy of hers. I've done everything I can to discourage it—"

"Like buying her the painting? Like reading her the Jack Rabbitt books?"

It was the flash of lightning he needed to set off his roar of thunder. "None of that was a problem until you and Blackstone offered to fulfill her wish."

"All children have fantasies."

"My kid doesn't. Not if I can help it."

She dared to approach. "Why are you so opposed to it?"

"Fantasies don't come true." Closer and closer still. So close he could smell her delicate fragrance. So close he could taste her sweet breath. "Fantasies are dangerous."

"They're dreams," she protested. "Harmless wishes."

His muscles bunched and he planted his hands on the butcher block, desperate to pounce. "Not all children have adults who appear like fairy godmothers and offer to bring those fantasies to life."

"Maybe they should! Maybe that's what Mathias knew that you didn't."

Tension vibrated through him and he drew himself up, a millisecond from taking her. Only gut instinct, held him in place for that vital extra moment, and he thanked all that was holy that, for once, he listened to that despised inner voice.

"Daddy?" River appeared in the doorway of the kitchen, her ever-present rag doll clutched protectively to her chest. "It's too noisy. I can't sleep." Her gaze shifted from one to the other, her eyes apprehensive and just a bit tearful. "I want Justice to tuck me in."

J.J. glanced at him and he nodded curtly. "Take her."

She gave River a gentle smile, a smile he'd kill to have turned his way, and held out a hand. "Come on, sweetie. I'd love to tuck you in."

Raven watched them go. With a groan, he leaned against the butcher block, his head lowered as he struggled for control. The storm swept past, screaming through him, leaving him buffeted and battered and totally exhausted.

But as always, it drained him of everything... everything except his guilt.

"Will you be here tomorrow when I wake up?" River asked, climbing onto her bed and slipping beneath the covers.

J.J. perched on the edge of her mattress. "Of course, I'll be here. I told you that at dinner."

"Promise?"

"I promise."

There was a long pause and then, "Dolly was afraid you might turn back into a fairy and fly away."

"Who's Dolly?"

River held up her rag doll. "Nawna made her for me. Nawna was my great-grandma. She died."

"Well, you tell Dolly that I won't leave without saying goodbye first."

"Promise?"

J.J. smiled at the childish ritual. "I promise."

"She won't leave, Dolly," River said, carefully straightening a black strand of the doll's yarn hair. "She promises."

J.J. pitched in, gently loosening the knots and smoothing the tangles. "Your grandmother did a beautiful job making her."

"Dolly's a fairy, too. Nawna sewed her up so she'd look just like you."

"Really?" The confession moved her unbearably. "That was a very sweet thing to do."

"Nawna even made Dolly wings. But I don't let her wear them very much."

"Why not?"

River nibbled on her lip. "I'm afraid she'll fly away."

"I don't think she'd do that," J.J. said gently. "She looks very happy to be with you. But it's okay to leave her wings off if you're worried. I'm sure Dolly doesn't mind."

Huge silver-blue eyes studied her anxiously. "Are your wings off?"

"Yes, sweetheart," J.J. reassured. "My wings are off. I'm not going anywhere until after I give you your wish."

River yawned, her eyes fluttering closed and she hugged Dolly. "Promise?"

"I promise."

J.J. sat in the darkened room for a while, watching as River drifted off to sleep. This couldn't continue. She and Raven were going to have to reach a truce for River's sake, if not their own. As soon as she was certain the little girl wouldn't wake, she slipped from the room.

Raven waited for her, a spent warrior exhausted from a particularly vicious battle. He handed her a scalding cup of coffee. "I see you've come to the same conclusion I have."

"Truce?" she asked dryly.

He nodded. "We don't have any choice. We can't keep locking horns or somebody's going to get hurt."

"I agree," she said, relieved. "Either we give River her wish or we end this."

He sipped his coffee, studying her through a haze of steam. "Are you willing to play the part of her mother for the next few days?"

A few days. A few weeks. She gazed up at Raven. A few years. She buried her nose in her mug. "I'll do my best."

His mouth tugged to one side. A mouth she'd taken great delight in kissing. A mouth that had consumed her with delicious ferocity. "No conditions, fairy lady?"

A thousand leapt to mind. "I'm too tired to think of any right now," she demurred. She hedged her bets, just to be on the safe side. "I'm sure I'll come up with one or two tomorrow."

He inclined his head. "Would you like another cup of coffee?"

Good heavens, had she emptied it already? "No, thanks. I'd like to sleep tonight." She placed her empty mug on a nearby table and took a quick breath. "Speaking of which…"

A devilish look sparked within his dark eyes. "You want me to put you to bed?"

"Raven—"

He relented. "There's a fold-out couch in the den."

"You have a den?" She didn't bother concealing her relief and he chuckled, the sound as rich and dark and delicious as the coffee he'd fixed.

"Off the living room. Did you really think I was going to force you to sleep with me?"

Yes, please. She shut her eyes so he wouldn't read the unspoken wish. She'd never felt so vulnerable before, so stripped of her usual protective veneer. "No, of course not," she said. But they both knew she lied.

"You *could* sleep with me."

The words hung between them, words that should never have been uttered. "Don't say it," she whispered. "Don't even suggest it. Neither of us is capable of that sort of affair. We're not casual people."

"We could make an exception."

"Take me to bed," an inner voice screamed. But aloud she forced herself to request, "Show me the den."

"Okay." He inclined his head toward the living room. "This way, Ms. Randell."

She latched onto the formality as though it were a lifeline. "Thank you, Mr. Sierra."

But he wasn't done tempting her. He caught her arm as she started past. Bending his head, his mouth brushed the curve of her cheek. "Just remember. You can change your mind. My door's always open."

The impact of his soft comment shivered through her. Carefully she eased from his hold. "I won't be walking through it," she insisted.

But she couldn't help wondering how long she'd be able to maintain that particular lie.

# CHAPTER SEVEN

Nemesis waited in his lair, sharply aware that his life hung in the balance. Soon he'd be forced to fight the prince—paying the ultimate price for a crime he hadn't committed.

Until recently, he'd assumed the battle was inevitable. But he'd just learned of a second quest, one which might insure his salvation. It offered him one small glimmer of hope in an otherwise bleak future.

A small fairy, an insignificant creature really, held his life within her hands. Small, soft, dainty hands. Though she didn't know it, she had the power to change his destiny. But only if her love was true.

Page 29, *The Great Dragon Hunt*
by Jack Rabbitt

"GOOD morning, Mommy!"

J.J. groaned at the far-too cheerful greeting and buried

her head deeper under a pillow. "It is *not* a good morning," she muttered crossly. Who had the unmitigated gall to talk to her at such an ungodly hour? And where the hell was her coffee? Check that. Where the hell was *she*?

"What's wrong with the morning?" The voice whined louder, darting in close to her ear with all the irritating persistence of a hungry mosquito. If she'd had the energy, J.J. would have whacked the pesky critter straight to Kingdom Come. "Mommy? Can't you talk? Are you awake? Mom-*my*?" The questions continued in a high-pitched, rapid-fire stream that the goose down comforter failed to block.

"Who are you?" J.J. growled, unable to bear the noise any longer. "Where am I?" One particular word nagged at her and she finally managed to key in on it. *Mommy.* "And why do you keep calling me Mommy?" As far as she could remember, she wasn't anyone's mother. At least, she didn't think so. At this horrendous hour, who could tell anything for certain?

"Don't you remember? I'm River. And you're Justice." The annoying voice came closer again and J.J. groaned. What she wouldn't give for a giant fly swatter. A nice, big, yard-long bug smacker. That would put a dent in Miss Cheerful's good cheer. "You came to be my Mommy for our vacation. You're a fairy. Don't you 'member?"

"I don't think so."

A brain cell or two came on-line and J.J. wedged open an eye. She peered out from beneath her pillow, squinting against the ruthless stab of sunlight. Damned sun. She glared at the little girl hovering nearby—an adorable sprite in a lacy nightie and a pair of inky braids. Man, did she hate "adorable" first thing in the morning.

"I know you," she admitted grudgingly. "I think."

The little girl whirled around, her perky little braids

flying in a circle around her equally perky little head.
J.J. grimaced. Jeez. Maybe it was perky she hated.

"Daddy, what's wrong with her?"

"Apparently fairies aren't too friendly first thing in
the morning. Give her a few minutes to wake up." The
deliciously masculine voice was connected to an equally
delicious odor. J.J.'s nose twitched. "I brought a magic
elixir that should help."

"What's a 'lixir?"

"A magic drink."

"Coffee," J.J. said with a moan.

She thrust a hand out from under her blanket and
snatched the proffered mug, retreating under the pillow
and blanket with it. It was the perfect temperature and
she didn't waste any time pouring it down her throat.
She thrust the empty mug into the middle of all that
horrible light and shook it, hoping the nice hand would
take it and fetch another helping of nice coffee.

"More," she demanded, just in case kind Mr. Hand
didn't understand the purpose of poor, empty Mr. Mug.

Mr. Hand turned nasty, taking Mr. Mug and relegating
him to the arctic netherlands of a nearby table. Damn!
If she ever got hold of Mr. Hand, he was gonna lose a
few Mr. Fingers.

"Really, Ms. Randell," the masculine voice murmured. "I told you to discourage the kid with a dose of
reality. But you didn't have to be quite so brutal about
it."

It took every ounce of willpower to keep from turning
the air blue with her retort. She settled for a mumbled,
"Go to hell."

His soft chuckle did more to wake her up than ten
cups of coffee. It rumbled ever so gently through the air.
Slipping beneath the covers, it seeped straight through
her skin, burrowing deep into the pit of her stomach. It
stayed there, warming her, teasing her toward wakeful-

ness. What would it be like to greet each day with such a delicious sound? Better than coffee—and she could have sworn there was *nothing* better than coffee first thing in the morning.

"Interesting." He approached, intensifying the warmth, turning up the heat to a fast, fierce burn. "Are we always so grumpy in the morning?"

She had to get rid of him before it got any hotter and she burst into flames. No telling what she'd do, if that happened. She'd become painfully susceptible to him, aroused by everything from his whiskey-rough voice to his soul-shattering touch. But first thing in the morning, before she'd had a chance to rebuild her defenses, having him this close was pure torture. It ought to be illegal. That way she wouldn't be tempted to turn amusing fantasy into delicious reality.

"No, *we* apparently are not grumpy in the morning. But *I* am. Now take your disgusting happy faces and get the h—" Her suggestion ended in a shriek as Raven ruthlessly stripped the blanket off her, exposing the silk boxers and skimpy cotton T-shirt she'd purchased for sleepwear. "What are you *doing?*"

His eyes caught fire as he saw what she wore—a fire that exactly mirrored the one scorching a path through her. Through. Over. In. Around. He exhaled harshly. "I'm waking up a grouchy fairy so she can start giving a little girl her wish."

Her memory finally came on-line. River. The wish. Raven. The kiss. "You told her?"

"Yup." His smile ate into her. "That way I could set the ground rules."

Ground rules? She knew his announcement should worry her, but she couldn't quite figure out why. "Don't you think you should have waited until I got up before letting her know?"

"After seeing what you're like first thing in the morning, I'm grateful I didn't.'' Wrapping a hand around her middle, he hoisted her off the couch. ''Up and at 'em, fairy lady.''

''Hey!'' Bent almost double, she tried to glare at him over her shoulder. A tousled black curtain of hair obscured her vision, thwarting her. She bicycled frantically through the air, getting nowhere fast. ''Let go!''

He lowered her a few tantalizing inches, allowing her toes to skim the carpet. ''What will you do if I put you down?''

''Go back to sleep, of course.''

''Wrong answer.'' He heaved her upward, his hands brushing the underside of her breasts.

''Don't you dare,'' she yelped.

''Oh, I dare,'' he retorted softly. ''You'd be amazed at how much I dare.''

River burst out laughing. ''Don't, Daddy. Don't put her down. Spin her around like you spin me.''

''Care for a spin, Ms. Randell?''

''*No!*''

''You can't call her Ms. Randell, Daddy. You have to call her Mommy.''

He hesitated for a split second and J.J. stopped struggling. ''She's not my mother, River.''

''Then call her Justice. And she can call you Raven. That's what Mommy called you, right?''

''I—'' Raven broke off, clearly unable to continue.

Slowly he eased J.J. to the floor. His arms still confined her, but a different sort of tension hummed through him—one precipitated by his daughter. His rapid breath tangled in J.J.'s hair and the muscles spanning his chest formed a rigid wall. His hands shifted, one settling on her hip, the other splayed across her abdomen. He eased forward while at the same time maneuvering her a tiny half step backward.

Her warmth collided with his. If she didn't know better she'd suspect having her in his arms afforded him a small measure of comfort. It was a ridiculous thought—but one that refused to fade.

Ever so gently, she slipped her hands across his, coupling their fingers, silently willing him some of her own strength.

At her touch, his voice broke loose. "Yeah, pumpkin. Your mother called me Raven."

River climbed onto J.J.'s bed and jumped up and down. "And honey. And sweetheart. And darling." She wrinkled her nose, her silvery-blue eyes alight with laughter. "Are you going to call Justice mushy names for vacation?"

"It's J.J., not Justice. And she isn't my wife."

Anguish ripped through his words and J.J. couldn't help herself. She turned ever so slightly and pressed a kiss to his chest. Her hair swept forward, hiding the compassionate act from River. But Raven felt it. He absorbed the gesture as if it were a blow, his muffled groan vibrating through them both. And then his tension eased, slipping away as though it had never been. His mouth drifted across the top of her head in silent thanks before he released her.

The bouncing grew more frantic. "Aren't you gonna pretend, too? You could pretend to be married and Mommy can be your wife and you can be the husban' and I'll be your little girl."

Raven snatched his daughter off the couch, holding her high overhead. "You *are* my little girl, silly puss."

Her bare feet thumped against his chest and he absorbed the kicks as though they were no more than a hail of snowflakes. "Come on, Daddy. Play the game. It's fun."

"You know I don't play games very well."

River sighed. "I know." She wrapped her arms

around his neck and gave him a fierce hug. "It's okay. I still love you."

His eyes closed. Emotions burst across his face leaving J.J. to feel as if she was the crassest of intruders. "I love you, too, baby."

She bit down on her lip. She'd never had that. Never had a father who'd held her in his arms and professed his love. Never had a husband who cherished her above all others. Never had a daughter to hug whenever the spirit moved her. It was a fantasy as illusory and impractical as River's wish. A dream she'd never experience.

Unexpected pain slashed her. "If you two will excuse me, I'll go shower and dress," she managed to say. "It won't take me long."

"And then we're going shopping. Right, Daddy? 'Cuz fairies can't go bare naked like in books. Not when they're real people."

Raven looked at J.J. over the top of his daughter's head. His eyes were blacker than the belly of a coal mine. But even as she watched, a distant light flickered to life in the deep recesses. What had caused it? she wondered helplessly. River? Memories of his late wife? Or perhaps a backwash of emotions, emotions too long suppressed. Whichever it was, something had clearly drawn him from that dark, lifeless place.

"You sure?" he murmured. "I don't mind having naked fairies flitting around the house."

Years of training came to J.J.'s rescue. To her profound relief, not a hint of warmth tinged her cheeks. "Too bad," she responded firmly. "This fairy will be wearing clothes."

And with that, she exited the room before River came up with any more brilliant ideas. But on her way to the bathroom, J.J. made the most distressing discovery. Somehow, somewhere, an impossible fantasy had slipped past her defenses, despite the rigorous safeguards she'd put in place. And that sweet, sweet fantasy had stolen her heart. Tears slipped down her cheeks, and she touched them in bewilderment. She never cried, couldn't recall the last time—

And then she remembered, remembered when she'd last felt the rain of tears on her face.

It had been the day she'd lost her mother. The day her fantasies had died.

Their shopping trip didn't get under way for a couple of hours. Breakfast and several cups of restorative coffee came first. Then chores and a few business-related phone calls. By the time they arrived in the small town of Snow Run, it was late morning.

"Where would you like to begin?" Raven asked, parking across from a pretty little square consisting of a string of gift shops and boutiques.

"How about there?" she replied promptly, pointing to a nearby clothing store. "Why don't we meet up with you in an hour or so? I think this might be a girls-only errand."

"You've forgotten one minor detail."

She couldn't mistake the deviltry in his black gaze. Suspicion seemed a justifiable reaction. "What?"

"I'm the one with the credit cards."

"Not a problem." J.J. offered a sweet smile. "I have my own plastic."

"And you'd be welcome to use it, except—"

Uh-oh. "Except what?" she asked fatalistically.

"Since I'm the one keeping you here longer than anticipated, I'm the one springing for your purchases." His words were as implacable as his expression.

"Mathias wouldn't expect—"

Raven wrapped an arm around her shoulder and pulled her into a loverlike embrace. He slid a hand deep into her hair, tilting her head so his mouth hovered mere inches above hers. River watched on, fascinated. "I'd like to make a suggestion, *wife*," he said in a voice too low for anyone else to hear. "Don't mention Blackstone to me. In case you didn't notice last night, it has a really bad effect on my temper."

"Daddy, are you going to kiss Mommy?" River questioned excitedly. "Are you going to play the game, too?"

His gaze shifted to her mouth and J.J. felt the breath shudder from between her lips. He must have felt it, too. "I'm tempted to find out if you taste as sweet as last time," he murmured.

"Don't get your hopes up," J.J. said in as steady a voice as she could manage. "Or River's, either. Remember? We're not supposed to be encouraging her fantasies."

"What about my fantasies?"

"I'm not here for you." She didn't mention Mathias, yet he might as well have been standing between them, his presence was that strong. "It's River's wish I'm fulfilling."

"Attempting to be practical, sweetheart?"

"I *am* practical. I've had to be."

"Time will tell."

He pivoted in a quick half-circle, his back to his daughter, his shoulders eclipsing her view. His mouth consumed J.J.'s in a devastatingly brief caress, the touch a potent blend of passion and hunger. Her lips clung for a fleeting instant, responding with an ardency she couldn't prevent. And then he released her.

"Tell me again how practical you are," he had the nerve to tease.

"As practical as you, apparently."

He grinned and she found it impossible to look away. It was a beautiful sight, his dark eyes brilliant with laughter, his face relaxed and open. For a wink of time the practical nature she'd been so certain she possessed deserted her. Impossible dreams seized her, offering tantalizing images of a life she'd secretly longed for since childhood. In that vision, Raven smiled at her all the time. He called her wife—and meant it—and River truly was their daughter.

The next moment, reality came crashing down. Dreams didn't come true, she reminded herself furiously. At least not for people like her. Calling herself every type of fool, she turned from enchantment's lure and held out her hand to River. "Come on, sweetheart. We have some serious shopping to do. And I'm going to need your help."

"Hey, fairy lady." Raven's voice chased after her on chill autumn winds.

She paused, unable to respond, her throat far too tight for speech. Hell, she couldn't even look at him.

He came up behind, dropping an arm around her shoulder. "Just so you know, you still taste as sweet as last time," he said gently. "Maybe even a bit more." And with that, he linked his fingers with hers, just as a real husband might.

The next few hours passed with amazing swiftness. Raven gave her a list of clothing she'd need while at the cabin—jeans, warm slacks, a down jacket, sweaters and a good dress.

"Oh, come on, Raven," she said, protesting the final item on his list. "What do I need that for?"

"We'll be going out to dinner at least one of the nights we're at the cabin. You'll need something dressy when we do."

"Perhaps you and your daughter would like matching outfits," the clerk suggested, no doubt sensing a nice, fat commission. "We have a number of lovely dresses to choose from."

Before J.J. could kill the woman, River piped up,

"Oh, Mommy, please?" She turned to Raven. "Can we, Daddy?"

J.J. half expected him to protest or show a hint of that ice-cold temper. Instead he stole her breath with a laugh. "An excellent idea."

"All little girls love to play dress-up," the clerk gushed. "And your daughter is an absolute miniature of your wife. Wait until you see. They'll look darling."

But this time J.J. put her foot down. "I think this is one outfit *Daddy* will have to miss previewing." She stooped beside River. "How about if we pick out our dresses and save them as a surprise."

Sure enough, the idea met with instant approval. "You can't peek, Daddy," River announced. "This is just for girls."

He started to turn away, but not before J.J. caught an odd expression slipping across his face. It took her a second to recognize the emotion he so swiftly masked. Sorrow, she realized with a touch of compassion. Sorrow that River's mother could never experience a moment like this with her daughter? It seemed likely. She pressed her lips together to keep them from trembling. Damn this wish! It had caused more trouble than it solved, baring vulnerabilities both of them had buried well and deep—painful memories neither wanted resurrected.

"Come on, Mommy. Let's pick out our dresses," River urged.

"Okay, sweetie." J.J. ruffled her "daughter's" hair. "What color are you in the mood for?"

Twenty minutes later, they'd completed their selection. The clerk quickly slipped the dresses into heavy black garment sacks. The rest of J.J.'s purchases had already been rung up and folded neatly into bags. Arms overflowing with purchases, the three returned to the Mercedes to stash everything in the trunk.

"Lunchtime," Raven announced, slamming closed

the lid. "There's a café around the corner that has great burgers and salads. Why don't we eat there?"

His suggestion met with an enthusiastic response. Fortunately wintertime tourists hadn't yet descended on the tiny ski town and they were shown a table right away. To J.J.'s surprise, she found herself relaxing over the meal. "You've really done a great job with her," she told Raven while River chattered with the waitress. "You should be very proud."

"Love, luck and a lot of patience."

"It couldn't have been easy for you."

"No. But I wasn't totally on my own. My grand-mother helped in the early days. She moved in with me and took care of River while I was at work." He hesi-tated a moment, then added, "She died last year."

"I'm sorry."

"Don't be. Nawna had quite a life. And she was a very spiritual woman. Death wasn't an ending for her, but a beginning."

"Is that how you feel, too?"

"Sometimes."

"And at others?" she asked softly.

"Other times I think we better deal with the here and now because that's all we're going to get." His mouth pulled to one side. "Of course, I knew better than to express that sort of attitude around my grandmother."

"I'll bet she'd have given you an earful."

"Without question."

The waitress finished her conversation with River and offered to take their order. After settling on a Caesar salad, J.J. glanced up to discover a couple at another table watching them. They smiled in a friendly fashion. Then the woman whispered to her companion, tapping a section of the newspaper spread between them. The two focused on her again and their smiles grew. J.J. averted her gaze self-consciously. Uh-oh. Looked as though Raven's announcement had hit the papers. She'd better make a point of snagging a copy before they returned to the cabin and see what had sparked their amusement.

Raven reached out and captured her hand. "I have one at home," he said quietly.

Startled, she switched her attention to him. "What?"

"The announcement that couple's smiling over," he replied without glancing in their direction. "I have a copy at the cabin. Or rather, Gem can call one up on the monitor for you."

"You noticed them looking at us?"

He shrugged. "You get used to it after a while."

"I'm not sure I could," she confessed in a troubled voice.

"Sometimes you don't have any other choice."

*He* hadn't had any choice after his wife died. Notoriety had been thrust on him. And in response, he'd built up a tough defense, refusing to allow anyone to touch him, or more likely to touch his daughter. Anyone who dared, would face his unique brand of vengeance. She shivered. Too bad Mathias had put her in that exact position. By attempting to have her fulfill this particular Christmas wish, he'd placed her squarely between Raven and his daughter. And Raven would do anything—*any-thing*—to protect the little girl from harm.

The first time she'd seen him, she'd caught a glimpse of the noble warrior that was such an intrinsic part of his personality. The only thing that had protected the reporters from his wrath had been the presence of his daughter—just as the only thing that had protected her from the full force of his fury had been River's intervention. J.J. could understand his feelings. If River were her daughter, she'd feel the same. But that knowledge brought home a disturbing truth.

Their battle hadn't concluded. Far from it. It had

merely been deferred until Raven determined whether or not she caused River any harm. And if she did...

The possibility haunted her through the rest of the meal.

The minute they returned to the cabin, J.J. carried her packages directly to the den. Raven had cleared out several desk drawers for her use, plus she'd discovered an empty closet where she could hang her new dress and jacket.

"Gem, are there any messages for me?" she questioned as she began removing her new wardrobe from the plastic bags and protective tissue.

"NEGATIVE, MS. RANDELL."

She glanced up and frowned. "Mathias hasn't phoned?"

"NO MESSAGES HAVE BEEN RECORDED."

What in the world was going on? Why hadn't Mathias returned any of her calls? Perhaps she should try reaching him at home again. She didn't want to worry Jacq considering her sister's baby was due in the next few weeks, but J.J. had to get instructions on how to handle her current predicament.

"Okay, no messages. How about a newspaper?" She pulled a black cashmere sweater with lustrous pearl buttons from one of the bags and a short, skin-tight suede skirt. Cashmere and suede? Now, when had these been chosen? She didn't even remember trying them on.

"AFFIRMATIVE, MS. RANDELL. NEWSPAPER MAY BE VIEWED ON MONITOR."

"Oh, that's great. Activate the screen, would you?" She plucked a skimpy handful of black silk and lace from another bag. What the...? Raven! It had to be. She certainly hadn't selected anything so patently sexy. She eyed the sweater and skirt. The undergarments would go beautifully with them, she admitted. Her new "husband" had quite an eye for women's clothing. "I'd like to see the announcement Mr. Sierra put in the paper today,'' she murmured absently.

''ONE MOMENT. ACCESSING.''

Carefully folding the sweater, she tucked it into a drawer along with the underwear. The TV flickered to life beside her and she rocked back on her heels to take a look. A newspaper clipping filled the twenty-four-inch screen, the huge words forming the headline practically leaping off the monitor at her. She had to read them twice before they sank in.

''Oh, no,'' she whispered in dismay.

*''SIERRA FULFILLS WISH!''*

J.J. groaned in disbelief as she scanned the headline, yet again. ''What has he done?'' She slowly rose and moved closer to the screen. It didn't get any better with proximity.

''Raven Sierra has announced his engagement to Seattle native, J.J. Randell,'' the clip read. ''The two were introduced when Sierra's five-year old daughter, River, expressed a 'wish' to meet the fairy who appears in the Jack Rabbitt line of storybooks. While press looked on, J.J. agreed to become the little girl's mother. At a picnic luncheon the next day, they discussed the possibility of wedding during their vacation. 'We haven't finalized our plans,' Sierra reports. 'This is too big a step for us to rush into. But my daughter is anxious to have J.J. for her mother. She even asked if we could ''pretend'' to be a family while on vacation.' No word on whether that particular wish has been fulfilled, though Sierra promises an update in the near future.''

J.J. didn't waste any time. She tore from the room, furious that she'd trusted him not to release a press announcement without examining it first. She couldn't even claim inexperience. After all the years she'd worked for her father's PR firm she, of all people, knew better.

She found him in the kitchen, preparing dinner. "How could you?" she demanded.

"I'll assume you've seen today's newspaper."

"Oh, I've seen it. I just don't believe it. You said you were going to announce our engagement, not—"

He cut her off with a single look. "I said I'd announce our engagement and do my best to spike Ms. Lark's guns. Or have you forgotten that minor detail?"

"I haven't forgotten a darned thing. Spiking that woman's guns does not include hanging Mathias out to dry. You said you'd keep this wish business a secret."

"I said I'd keep Blackstone's name out of it. And I did."

"But you told about the wishes!"

"Ms. Lark overheard River discussing her wish. I had to address it. And the best way of doing that is sticking as close to the truth as possible."

"Mathias—"

He slammed the point of his knife into the cutting board. It stuck, quivering from the impact. She shifted her gaze from the knife to his fierce black eyes and fought to draw breath. He would *not* intimidate her. She wouldn't allow it. No man would ever intimidate her again. She stepped closer to the cutting board and planted her hands on either side of the knife. Then she leaned across it toward him.

"You're going to ruin your knife point doing that, not to mention gouging the cutting board."

He thrust a hand through his hair, the dark waves stubbornly falling across his brow. The muscles in his jaw leapt as he fought for control. Finally he nodded. "I apologize. That was uncalled for. I'm not exactly rational when it comes to your boss."

"I swear to you, he's not trying to hurt River."

"And I intend to make certain of it. That announcement in the newspaper is my warning salvo. I arranged for Gem to send it to him. If he pushes me about the painting or causes my daughter so much as a moment's discomfort, I'll give the press a real scoop about the nature of that wish. I expect Blackstone will read between the lines and understand what I'm saying."

A terrible suspicion took hold. "Have you been intercepting his calls to me?"

"No."

"Would you tell me if you had?"

"Yes."

Fair enough. She'd been around enough dishonest men to know when they were lying. Mathias might be ruthless, but he didn't strike her as dishonest. In fact, he seemed compellingly straightforward. "So now you've warned Mathias. Where does that leave us?"

"It leaves us sharing a vacation together for the next few days and fulfilling my daughter's wish." His eyes were as black as pitch. "We don't have much time left. So I suggest we focus on our true purpose."

"And once it's over?"

"You return to Seattle and stay out of our lives."

It was implacably stated, without a hint of the emotions she'd come to expect. And it hurt, more than she could have anticipated. But what had she expected? A declaration of love? Gently she freed the embedded knife and set it carefully on the cutting board.

"I believe that's another wish I can grant," she replied with utter calm. "No extra charge."

It was the best exit line she'd get, and one she didn't delay taking advantage of.

# CHAPTER EIGHT

Justice stood before Fausta, the silk bag at her waist containing five of the seven gifts intended for Nemesis. Capturing each of the four elements had been difficult enough. But she suspected obtaining the final two objects would be the most challenging of all.

Compassion glittered in the older fairy's eyes. "Yes, young one. You're right. Finding the last two gifts will be an arduous task. For you must offer the dragon something belonging to you— and something belonging to your prince."

Justice smiled. That didn't sound too hard. "Like a piece of clothing or jewelry?"

"No, my dear. Your gift must be of yourself. A gift only you could give."

Page 34, *The Great Dragon Hunt*
by Jack Rabbitt

TIME was passing with a swiftness J.J. found frightening. River had created a dream world for them, one whose allure they all found irresistible. But like most dreams and fantasies, it would soon end. How would they react once it did? J.J. wondered uneasily. How would *she* react?

Not well, she suspected. Not considering she'd given herself, heart and soul, into her "family's" keeping.

The third day at the cabin Raven suggested they go for a hike and explore some of the surrounding trails. The weather had changed from frosty to warm—typical of early fall in these parts, he'd revealed. Even snow was a possibility, though it wouldn't last long at this time of year. To J.J.'s amusement, River insisted on looking for dragons during their hike, examining leaves and shrubs for "dragon-sign."

"You can smell them," she explained for Raven's benefit. "And they burn the woods. That's how you know they live nearby."

"Really?" he questioned dryly. "Here I thought it was lightning strikes and careless campers that caused most fires."

"And all along it was your friendly neighborhood dragon," J.J. murmured. "Silly you."

At one point, Raven stopped to show River a cut in the mountainside from a long-ago landslide. "See all the layers," he said, pointing to the colorful diagonal lines of earth. "Each one is from a different age."

"Which age has the dragons and fairies?" River demanded, squatting beside her father to peer at the exposed strata.

"No dragons," he replied with a sigh. "And no fairies. But some of these layers were from the age of the dinosaurs."

"Which ones?"

He pointed. "That's about a hundred million years ago. And this is even older." He ran a finger along a bed farther down. "This section actually has a name. It's called the Morrison Formation. It's a hundred and forty million years old. It's easy to find because of this bunch of lines right here. See how they go back and forth from purple to gray to almost green? Those are layers of shale and clay."

"I have clay," River volunteered. "I make animals with it."

"Well, this is just like your modeling clay, except better, because it's so much older."

River stilled, her breath hitching. "Is this special earth, Daddy?"

"Sure is. Most places you'd have to dig down very deep to find something this old."

She clasped her hands together, her eyes alight with excitement. Now what had brought that on? J.J. wondered curiously.

"Can I have some of the special dirt?" River pleaded. "Can I take it home?"

"I guess. This part looks like it's going to wash down the hillside with the next rain, anyway. So it shouldn't hurt if you take a small piece. But just this once. It's best to leave everything the way we find it so other hikers can enjoy the sights, too."

"Just this once," River was quick to assure. "I promise."

Carefully he scooped up a small sampling of the brittle shale and a softer section of clay and wrapped it in a leaf. "That should keep it safe until we're home. Be careful you don't get it wet because it'll turn sticky. Maybe we should put it in a plastic baggy so we don't have dinosaur dirt tracked all over the house."

River threw her arms around her father's neck. "Oh, thank you! This is the best walk ever."

He lifted an eyebrow. "It is, huh?" He shot J.J. a baffled glance. "I'll take your word for it."

"Now I need to find some special water." She pulled back, tilting her head to one side. Hero worship gleamed in her eyes. "Do you think you can find that, too?"

He frowned. "What the heck is 'special' water?"

"It's like special earth, only water," River replied, matter-of-factly.

"Okay. Well... If I find any, you'll be the first to know."

"What do you need it for?" J.J. couldn't help asking.

River's eyes widened with a hint of alarm. "I just do."

"But, why?"

"Because." She didn't like being pressed, that much was clear. "Because it's a game," she said, and then took off down the path.

"River, wait for us," Raven called.

She paused at a bend in the trail and waved to them. "Come on. Hurry up. Maybe we'll find some water over here."

The fourth day arrived all too soon. After an exhausting game of hide-and-seek, the three returned to town for a movie and window-shopping. But River seemed restless, distracted. Now in addition to asking that they help her find special water, she also asked endless questions about the wind.

"River, for the last time, I don't know how to catch wind in a bottle," Raven said, his patience shot.

"But you have to!" she stormed at him. "You know everything."

"I'm flattered you think so. Unfortunately you've managed to uncover the one skill I lack. I don't know how to bottle wind." He frowned as he eyed his daughter's unhappy expression. "I'm sorry. I wish I did, sweetheart."

River didn't respond, but the mutinous set of her chin spoke volumes.

"Can't you tell me what you need it for?"

Stubbornly, she shook her head. "It's a secret."

"Keeping secrets is very important," J.J. interrupted, exchanging a worried look with Raven. "So long as they're good secrets. Is this a good one? Will it make someone happy?"

"It's the best secret ever." River threw herself against J.J. It was a silent plea for comfort, a child hurting and desperate for someone to take the pain away.

J.J. held her close. "And your secret won't harm anyone?" she probed.

River hesitated. "Not unless the dragon eats me," came her muffled response. "That's why I need the wind and the water."

"To protect you from the dragon?" Raven demanded. The clipped way he asked the question underlined his displeasure at the direction her answers had taken.

"No. To *give* to the dragon. It's a present."

Her father stooped beside her. "Who is this dragon, River?"

"You know. Nemesis."

"And have you...*seen* Nemesis?" he persisted.

"I looked and looked, but I didn't find him." She lifted her head. "I need to get all the presents before Justice leaves and give them to him. Otherwise it won't work."

"I don't understand," J.J. said, smoothing silken hair from River's brow. "What won't work? Why do you need to give the dragon presents?"

But no amount of probing would get her to say more. Forcing the issue only provoked tears.

"I'll see what I can do to help find your presents, okay?" Raven finally said, his forbearance stretched to the limits. "Will that do?"

River eased from J.J.'s embrace. "Before Justice leaves?"

His mouth tightened. "I'll try. That's the best I can offer."

Resigned, if not entirely satisfied, River nodded. "Okay." Tugging free of J.J.'s arms, she ran to a nearby shop window and pressed her nose to the glass.

"What the hell is going on?" he asked, the minute she'd moved beyond earshot.

"I think she's acting out some sort of game."

He frowned. "Is it something in that book you gave her?"

"I don't know," J.J. confessed. "I haven't read it."

"Nor have I." His eyes narrowed. "In fact, I haven't seen it in days."

"Did you bring it to the cabin?"

"Damned if I remember." He studied River for a moment longer, his frown deepening. "Well, whatever this game is, it's not one I like."

J.J. caught his hand and gave it a quick, reassuring squeeze. "Are you okay?" she asked gently.

He summoned a smile. "Just a bit bruised from falling off my pedestal. I'll recover."

"Don't worry. She'll have you right back up there before long."

But to their joint concern, River didn't recover her good humor.

On the fifth day all three of them felt the burden of time's passage, a fact beautifully demonstrated by a rash of temper tantrums and tears—most of them as a result of the announcement that their vacation would soon end.

J.J. knew she had to act. She'd come to give a little girl a special wish and she'd make sure she'd done her utmost to fulfill it before returning to Seattle. "Well, if we don't have much time left," she said to River, "we'd better hurry."

"Hurry and do what?" The question was accompanied by a loud sniff.

J.J. offered a mysterious smile. "Oh, I have all sorts of fun projects planned."

There were so many activities she'd love to do with her "daughter" and so little opportunity in which to accomplish them. These past few days had been some of the most incredible she'd ever experienced, as much a fantasy-come-true for her as for River. It devastated J.J. to realize their time together would soon end.

She held out her hand. "Come on, sweetie. Let's get started."

The first order of business was making fans. "Your daddy said we're going to a fancy restaurant tomorrow night, so fans are a must," she informed River. "Do you know how to make them?"

River shook her head, wide-eyed. But she quickly got into the spirit of things when J.J. showed her how to color a piece of construction paper and then fold it into long, narrow sections. The first few attempts were discarded as unworthy. But eventually River settled on a design she liked—a drawing of Nemesis on one side and a close-up of his glowing green eyes and red-hot breath on the other.

Next they decorated their creations with sequins and glitter and tiny seed pearls J.J. had purchased on their last shopping expedition. Once the glue had dried, they carefully folded their artwork into the proper shape. As a finishing touch, painted and glitter-bedecked Popsicle sticks were attached to each end for added reinforcement.

"See what Nemesis does when I wave him?" River asked, flipping the scalloped paper back and forth. Green sequined eyes and fire red glitter flashed with each wave.

J.J. chuckled, waving her creation at River. "Oh, yeah? Well, take that."

It started an instant war to see who could cause the biggest breeze. River ran circles around J.J. waving her fan and shrieking in laughter as the air currents wove her "mother's" hair into an unmanageable tangle.

"Okay, okay! You win," J.J. proclaimed at last, holding up her hands in surrender. "Good grief, River. I look like I've been through a windstorm."

The little girl froze, staring at J.J. in amazement, her expression one of joyous excitement. "They're wind makers!"

"What?"

"My fan. I can make the wind with them. Oh, Justice!" River threw herself into J.J.'s arms. "Thank you! Thank you! I needed this."

J.J. shook her head in bewilderment. "Well…great. Then I'm glad I suggested it. You don't need wind in a bottle anymore?"

"No. Now all I have to get is some special water."

"Which I don't have," J.J. said regretfully.

"That's okay. Daddy will help me find it." She wrapped her arms around J.J.'s waist. "So what are we going to do next?"

"Next, we bake cookies. Have you ever done that before?"

To her astonishment, River shook her head. Poor kid. Five years old and she'd never experienced the joy of making a batch of cookies with her own two hands.

"I don't know how to make them," she explained with heart-wrenching sincerity. "Just how to eat them."

"I'll bet you're really good at that," J.J. teased.

"The best."

They went off in search of Raven, insisting he join in their next project. It didn't take much pleading. Before long all three of them were swathed in aprons and elbow-deep in cookie dough. Flour soon covered the table, floor and chairs. And chocolate chips and brown sugar had found homes in some very intriguing spots around the kitchen. Not that it mattered. Seeing River laugh again, her good humor restored, made it all worthwhile.

The timer went off, announcing the completion of their first culinary attempt and J.J. crossed to the oven, removing an aluminum sheet full of lightly browned chocolate chip cookies. While she transferred them onto a strip of waxed paper, River and Raven continued working side by side to get the next batch ready.

"Come on. Quit goofing off," he ordered in mock-annoyance. "We're falling behind. And stop eating the dough. That's supposed to be for the cookies."

River's expression turned devious. "It was an accident. My finger fell in the bowl all by itself."

"Well, it can get out all by itself, too."

"Okay," she said, pulling her hand away from temptation. That lasted a whole five seconds. "Oh, no. Help, help! Now my pinkie fell in."

Raven lifted an eyebrow. "Oh, yeah? Well, you tell your pinkie to climb right back out of there or I'll bake it up with the cookies. Yum. Chocolate chip pinkies. My favorite."

"Okay, she's out," came the muffled reply.

J.J. grinned. Apparently Miss Pinkie had jumped from the cookie dough straight into a hungry little mouth. She waited for the inevitable follow-up. It wasn't long in coming.

"Oh, no. Now my thumb fell in. And look! All the other fingers are sliding in, too!"

Raven shook a wooden spoon at his daughter. "You tell that thumb and all her friends to get out of the cookie dough or else."

"Or else what?"

"Or else your little backside is going to meet up with Daddy's big, bad hand."

River giggled. "You're teasing me." She erupted from her chair and threw herself into his arms, patting his cheeks with sticky fingers. "You know you won't spank me."

"Maybe not," he admitted, sighing in resignation over the cookie dough beard she'd given him. "But I will plant your backside on your bed if you don't behave."

"No, Daddy. That's only when I'm *really* bad." Her brows drew together. "Is falling in the cookie dough *really* bad?"

"No. Just sort of bad." He wrinkled his brow in thought. "Well… Maybe not sort of, either. But it's a lot silly."

"Silly's okay, right?"

A slow smile spread across his face. "Yeah. Silly's just fine."

She pressed a chocolate-coated kiss to his cheek, adding to his doughy beard. "I love you, Daddy."

He hugged her, his eyes falling shut, his expression almost painful to witness. "I love you, too, pumpkin."

J.J. blinked away tears, more moved than she could have imagined. Apparently Raven's place on his daughter's pedestal had been recovered. The knowledge brought a tremulous smile to her lips.

Their sixth day at the cabin arrived and then waned into afternoon. And with its passing came the knowledge that they only had one more day to spend as a family. Tomorrow would be their last.

"But at least we get to go out to dinner in a few hours." J.J. attempted to console a devastated River.

That sparked a little interest. "Can we wear our matching dresses?"

"Absolutely. And we'll fix our hair, too."

"And put on makeup?"

It was bribery at its most blatant, but J.J. didn't have the heart to refuse. "And wear makeup." She held up her thumb and index finger pinched close together. "A little bit of makeup." Somehow she didn't think Raven could handle more than that.

"How will you fix my hair?"

"I thought we'd make braid crowns."

"What's a braid crown?"

J.J. bit down on her lip. Poor Maise. She'd missed out on so many special times with her daughter. So many joyous moments that little girls remembered all their lives—remembered and passed down to their own daughters.

"Why don't we get started right now? That way I can show you what they are."

River clasped her hands together in excitement. Perching on the edge of her bedroom chair, she held perfectly still while J.J. brushed out her hair. "Are you going to braid it? Daddy braids it a lot."

"I sure am. But first we need ribbons. Let's see…" She opened the bag of goodies she'd bought at the same time as the materials for the fans and pulled out a handful of gold ribbons. "I need to weave these in while I braid your hair."

River's brow wrinkled. "How did you learn this?"

Deftly J.J. began working the braids. It had been a long time since she'd attempted this particular hairstyle, but to her relief, it came back with amazing ease. "My mother used to make braid crowns for my sister, Jacq, and me."

"Was your mommy a fairy, too?"

J.J.'s mouth trembled into a smile as sweet memories winged through her mind. "She was a fairy queen and she made all our lives magical." Tying off the braids, she wrapped them around River's head and pinned them in place. "Now look."

River's gasp of delight was all the reward J.J. could have wanted. "I look…" Tears sparkled in her eyes. "I look beautiful."

"Yes, you do. Wait until your daddy sees you."

River insisted that J.J. fix her hair in a braid crown, too. "So we'll match. Like a *real* mommy and her little girl."

"Okay. But you have to help." She couldn't resist dropping a kiss on River's brow. "That's how it works with mommies and their little girls."

It took time, but sheer grit and determination helped compensate for fumbling fingers and lopsided braids. The eventual crown wasn't perfect, but J.J. wouldn't have changed the final results for anything in the world.

And then came makeup. Again River held utterly still—chin raised and lips pursed. J.J. touched the alabaster cheeks with blush, the bowed lips with a hint of pink lipstick, and the upturned nose with a fine dusting of powder. Again, River ran to the mirror. She stared for a long time and J.J. couldn't help thinking she was drinking in the experience, filing it away so she'd always remember.

Finally came their dresses—fairy-tale creations in a soft, shimmery gold satin with high waists, puffed sleeves and squared necklines. "Only one final touch," J.J. announced. Reaching into her bag of goodies she pulled out two jewelry boxes. She handed one to River. "Go ahead, sweetheart. Look inside."

Trembling with excitement, River pried open the velvet box. Inside she found a heart-shaped gold locket nestled in a bed of white satin. "Is this for me?" she whispered in disbelief.

"It's my gift to you." J.J. fought for composure. "You know I have to leave soon. But I thought you could have this to remember me by.'' She showed River how to open it. "See? It has a lock of my hair. Anytime you miss me, all you have to do is—'' To her utter horror, her voice broke.

River threw herself into J.J.'s arms. "I love you, Mommy. Please don't leave.''

It was a fight to reply with the tears blocking her throat. "I have to.''

"Would you stay if you could?''

*In a heartbeat.* She drew a deep, shuddering breath. "I can't.''

"But would you, if you could?''

She hugged River close, refusing to lie. After all, fairies couldn't lie. "You know I would.'' She drew back, brushing away tears with shaking fingertips. "I didn't show you what else I bought.''

She opened the other jewelry box to reveal another locket—a perfect match for River's. "This way I can remember you, too.''

"Will you put my hair in yours?''

"I'd love to.''

"Do it now,'' River urged.

It only took a few minutes to unwrap her braids and trim off a tiny snippet of hair. J.J. secured it in her locket and fastened the gold chain around her neck. Then she gathered up their fans. They practiced fluttering them, giggling at their own silliness before J.J. tied them to their wrists with the remaining gold ribbons.

"Are you ready? I'm sure it's past time to go downstairs. Your poor daddy is probably wondering what happened to us.''

"I'll tell him we were being girls. That's what he always says when I take too long getting ready.''

J.J. nodded, fighting tears again. "We sure were being girls. And I bet he'll love the result.'' And then they joined hands and left the room.

*        *        *

Raven paused in the hallway, unable to do anything but stand and stare. J.J. and River were poised at the top of the staircase. And they took his breath away. In that brief moment he felt the irresistible lure of fantasy. *This could be real,* it whispered into his ear. *You could have this if you just believe.* And he wanted it to be real. Wanted it desperately.

"Look at us," River called to him. "Don't we look beautiful?" J.J. bent with a rustle of satin and whispered something into her ear and she nodded. "I mean... How do we look, Daddy?"

"You look beautiful. Stunning," he assured her roughly. And heaven help him— "All grown up."

They descended the steps, joining him in the hallway. "Is it time to go?" J.J. asked.

"Not quite. We've got a small problem." He crossed to the front door and tugged it open, sweeping a hand toward the darkness outside. Snow fell in a thick white curtain.

River caught her breath in a gasp. "It's snowing!" A careless gust sent a small whirlwind spinning in through the open doorway and she chased it, trying to capture the flakes in her hands. They caught in her braids instead, white pinpricks against a sable backdrop, before melting, leaving behind the sparkle of diamond droplets.

"The first snow of winter," Raven confirmed. "You asked for special water, River. Here it is."

"How beautiful," J.J. whispered.

"What do I put it in? Quick, Daddy. I have to catch the snow."

J.J. snapped her fingers. "I have a small bottle upstairs. It had a sample of shampoo in it. But it's almost empty. We could clean it out and fill it with snow."

"Can we do it now, before we go to dinner?" River pleaded.

"I'm afraid that's the bad news," Raven interrupted.

"The roads are a mess. We're going to have to stay home tonight."

"That doesn't mean we can't have a special dinner," J.J. hastened to say.

He smiled. "Don't worry. It's already taken care of."

As soon as he'd realized they weren't going into town, he'd made alternate arrangements. The first order of business had been to move the kitchen table into the living room, right next to a roaring fire. During a brief foray outside, he'd collected cedar boughs, pinecones and berries and dumped them into a large wooden bowl. As a final touch, he'd stuck a couple of candles in the middle of the arrangement. As a centerpiece, it wasn't perfect, but it would do. Next, he'd tossed a couple Cornish game hens into the oven with some carrots and baby red potatoes. If the odor wafting through the cabin was any indication, dinner was almost ready.

"What can we do to help?" J.J. asked, looking around.

He waved her toward the living room. "Just have a seat. I've got everything under control."

"Let's turn off all the lights and just use the candles," River suggested.

Raven frowned. "Hang on. I'll have to find some matches. I seem to have misplaced my lighter." He shook his head. "First my cuff links and now this."

The dinner turned out to be a huge success—warm and leisurely, interspersed with plenty of laughter. After they'd eaten, Raven moved the table back to the kitchen and spread a wool blanket in front of the fireplace. Then they all played cards by candlelight, the hours slipping by. Finally, exhausted, River curled up on one corner of the blanket, her braid crown tumbling over one eye. With a small yawn, she drifted off to sleep.

"I'll take her up and be back in a minute," Raven murmured.

Gently he lifted his daughter into his arms and carried her off. But he soon discovered J.J. didn't wait for him downstairs. Instead he found her in his room. As he entered, she bent toward the hearth by his bed and set a burning match to the stack of wood he'd laid earlier. The fire caught, shedding the reflection of its glittering flame across the paleness of her skin. Satisfied, she sat back. Her skirt surrounded her in a circle of rippling satin and he couldn't help thinking she looked like a fairy perched in the middle of a pool of gold.

She turned her head toward him. Her eyes were dark in the firelight, threaded with just a hint of amber. "Did you get River to bed?"

It was such a prosaic question, it made him smile. It also brought home the reminder that fantasy and reality rarely intersected—and the few times they did, there was invariably a collision.

"She's sound asleep. I tucked Dolly in next to her in case she wakes up in the middle of the night."

"Does she do that often?"

"No." He waited a moment and when she didn't say anything further, he asked, "Is something wrong?"

"No. Yes." She laughed, the sound deep and husky. Emotional. Revealing. "I'm just sitting here, struggling to reach a decision."

"Is it a decision I can help with?"

"Not really. It's one I need to make for myself."

He stepped closer. "But it involves me." He didn't bother asking. The answer was self-evident.

Her mouth trembled into a slow smile. "Yes. It involves you."

With a tiny sigh of resignation—or perhaps inevitability—J.J. lifted her arms and unclasped the locket from around her neck. Ever so gently, she set it on the hearth. It flickered in the firelight, capturing the fiery dance within its metallic heart before reflecting it outward. He waited to see what she'd do next. She didn't keep him in suspense for long.

She reached behind her, the precision of her movements unexpectedly elegant. The rasp of her zipper rent the heavy silence, followed by the whisper-soft swish of satin. Her dress slid from her shoulders and collapsed, baring her to the waist.

Raven fought to draw breath. "I assume you've reached your decision."

"Oh, yes."

It was such a simple response, but one that threatened to shatter him. She stood with infinite grace, rising from the golden pool of satin as if she were a glorious sea nymph emerging from sun-blissed waves. She wore very little—silk stockings, held in place with lace garters, a scrap of silk at the juncture of her thighs and Eve's smile.

"And now it's your turn to decide," she said.

# CHAPTER NINE

Justice had all her gifts but one—the prince's contribution. But he'd disappeared. She'd searched all of Fairy for him. Everywhere, except the hidden lair of Nemesis.

Gathering her courage, she slipped through the forest until she stood just outside the entrance to the dragon's cave. And there she found the prince, his sword poised, ready to pierce the heart of the mighty Nemesis.

"No," the fairy cried. "Don't kill him. For if he dies, our dreams die with him."

> Page 37, *The Great Dragon Hunt*
> by Jack Rabbitt

RAVEN couldn't take his eyes off J.J. Ever so gently he closed the door to his bedroom. "Gem?"

"PROCEED."

"Alert me if River leaves her room tonight."

"AFFIRMATIVE."

J.J. tipped her head to one side. She'd combed out her braids, and her hair cascaded like spilled ink across one shoulder. It cupped the outer curve of her pale breast as if it were a lover's hand. "Shall I assume you've reached your decision, Mr. Sierra?" She offered a brave smile, as though his response wasn't of critical importance. But her eyes held a smoky darkness that reminded him of a carefully banked ember—an ember needing only a wisp of life-giving air to bring it back to full flame.

"Come here."

She walked toward him, every step sheer seduction. And she didn't stop until the coral tips of her breasts grazed his shirt. "Make certain," she said. "Make very certain this is what you want."

"I was certain the minute you walked into my life." Ever so gently, he took her into his arms, enclosing her in warmth.

She lifted her face and with a small sigh, covered his mouth with hers. In that instant, realization dawned. Waves of understanding spread through him, growing ever stronger, ever more certain with each passing minute. J.J. offered something he'd never had before—never expected to have. She gave him the whole of her spirit. She gave him utter trust. And she gave him fulfillment.

He finally understood what his grandmother meant about a "gold spirit." It wasn't just J.J.'s goodness or the way she put others before herself. In fact, it wasn't noble self-sacrifice he'd witnessed at all. She simply gave *of* herself—her love, her time, her attention. She took incompletion and completed it.

She closed circles.

How different from his former wife. Maise had constantly chased fulfillment outside their marriage. He'd never had a sense that she found it with him, despite the love they'd felt for each other. Perhaps if she had, she wouldn't have been so bent on exploring every New Age craze that came along, or standing outside in a thunderstorm growing a deadly case of pneumonia. He'd never been enough for her. For the first time, Raven recognized that fact. Recognized, and accepted it, despite the sadness it wrought.

"What is it?" J.J. whispered, breaking off their kiss. "What's wrong?"

"I was saying good-bye."

Comprehension lit her gaze. "To Maise."

"Yes."

"You loved her very much, didn't you?"

"She was my life," he said simply. "She was the first woman I ever truly loved."

"The newspapers got it wrong."

"They got it wrong," he confirmed.

Her eyes gathered him up, branded him with a heat he could feel all the way to his marrow. "Are you sure this is what you want?" she asked.

He could practically taste her compassion. "Lady, I want to make love to you more than anything."

"I'm not Maise," she warned.

"And Maise wasn't you."

"In that case..." Her smile quivered to life. "I believe you're wearing too many clothes."

"There's a simple solution." He offered himself up to her kind generosity. "Take them off me."

The husky demand brought her smile to full ripeness. But for the first time she showed a slight hesitation. He almost laughed out loud. She stood before him in all her natural glory and yet exhibited a virginal shyness about removing his clothing.

"If you want to make love, I'm afraid they have to come off," he ever-so-gently teased.

Taking a deep breath, she reached for his neckline, tugging at his tie. So deliberate, so careful. Finally unknotting it, she pulled, sliding the silk length from around his collar. She tackled the buttons next. Slow. Dainty. One button at a time, until his shirt fell open. He held out his wrists and she removed the cuff links he'd used as a replacement for River's. His shirt drifted to the carpet. She paused, sparing a moment to run her hands across his chest, measuring the breadth of his shoulders and strength of his biceps.

He shuddered beneath the delicate touch. "Don't stop there," he urged.

She reached for his belt buckle and stilled. It was then his gut instinct kicked in—the one he'd always assured Nawna he didn't possess. And he knew…knew the truth, even though he'd have thought it impossible. "You've never done this before, have you?"

Her laugh shivered between them. "No."

"Why now?" he demanded. "Why with me?"

Her eyes flickered, clashing with his, full-on. "You're the first man I trust. The one man who's right for me. You…complete me, instead of trying to control me."

It was his own words given back to him. As true for her as they were for him. He ripped the comforter off his bed and spread it in front of the fire. "Lie down," he urged. Sensing her nervousness, he gave her a kiss of reassurance, offering a brief taste of the passion he struggled so hard to hold in check. "Trust me. When we make love I want it to be special, as well as safe."

It only took a moment to shed his trousers and retrieve a protective packet from his dresser drawer. Grabbing an armload of pillows, he scattered them around the comforter before lowering himself beside her. He opened his arms to her, relieved when she flew into them. It was then he realized he'd been holding his breath, expecting her to have second thoughts.

"You don't have to worry," she said softly. "I won't ask you to stop."

He lifted an eyebrow. "Reading my thoughts? Is that an example of fairy magic?"

"No. It doesn't take any magic to know that you're one of those who fights the good fight." She stirred within his arms, looking up at him in utter seriousness. "You'd never take advantage of a situation. In fact, I suspect you'd go to the other extreme. If I'd changed my mind, you'd feel honor-bound to stop."

His mouth twisted. "Death before dishonor?"

"Yes," she whispered. "Especially since you've discovered that dishonor is worse than death."

He clenched his teeth. "Is that really how you see me? A man who's lost his honor?"

How could she possibly know how he'd felt about Maise's death? He'd blamed himself a thousand times over for not protecting her better, lived through the guilt and remorse that mistake had wrought. How could she possibly understand? And yet...somehow she did.

"I didn't say you were dishonorable. But you've had your good name stripped from you by people like Ms. Lark." He couldn't deny it, and she continued with an empathy that threatened to destroy him. "You're a man who's fought too many wars, unwilling to return home for fear he'll find all he holds dear long gone."

Her comment cut to the quick. He knew she spoke spiritually, which only made it more painful. She was right. He was afraid to look too deeply at his life, afraid he'd discover nothing at the core but a dark void. "And how would you know that?" His voice grated, raw with pain—a dead giveaway.

She shifted, kneeling within the circle of his arms, her gaze locking with his. The firelight warmed the honey in her eyes and burnished her cheekbones with a vibrant glow. Reaching up, she cupped his face, her touch offering a succor he'd never before possessed. "Because I've known dishonor. And because I'm afraid to go home, too. You're not alone, Raven. I'm with you every step of the way.''

With an anguished groan, he bent to her, drinking in her taste, allowing her sweetness to drive the poison from his soul. Every kiss became a healing balm, every touch a rejuvenation of spirit. And when she'd given all she had, he gave back, worshiping her with all that was in him, doing his utmost to make this a moment she'd remember for the rest of her life.

Gently he eased her backward onto the comforter. Her hair pooled beneath her head like a midnight tide and he sank his hands into the rippling waves of darkness, marveling at the softness. He joined them with a kiss, spreading her lips and easing within, losing himself in a pleasure more intense than any he'd ever known.

Beside him a log crackled and sparks sprayed upward. It was a raging fire trapped behind an iron grate. Raven lifted his head and stared down at J.J. A similar fire raged within him. But the woman in his arms had removed the grate and loosened the flames, allowing them to consume all in their path. Allowing them to consume her, as well.

She was the most perfect woman he'd ever seen, her limbs long and lean, her breasts high and firm, the peach-hued tips puckered for his kiss. He caught them between his teeth feeling the tension building in the fluid muscles beneath his hands, a preliminary rippling of passion. He reached for the swell of her hips, slipping the scrap of silk down her legs. And once he'd stripped the last of her clothing away, he kissed a trail of fire upward, anointing her sweetness until she cried for him—cried a song more alluring than a siren's.

Desire didn't unfurl, but exploded, generating a heat to rival the fire's core. He saw the shock in her eyes, swiftly replaced by a desperate need. She bunched the comforter in her fists, opening herself to him in a silent plea. He slid his hands beneath her and angling her hips upward, poised above. In that timeless moment, their gazes meshed. She'd called him a warrior, described him as a man of honor. But there was one thing she hadn't said. One word she hadn't used. That omission glowed in her eyes. In that brief instant she surrendered the last bit of herself, hiding nothing from him, forcing him to acknowledge the truth.

When she gave herself to him it was out of love. And when he took her and made her his own, he gave back that love a hundred fold.

Raven handed J.J. a glass of wine before tossing another log on the fire. They'd slept for a short time after they'd made love, but neither wanted to waste the evening on such a prosaic pastime as sleep. Not when there were so many more interesting activities.

"So tell me, fairy lady," he said. "Why are you so certain you're the practical one in your family?"

She sat up, wrapping an arm around her bent knee. Her dark hair caped her shoulders in satin. "It's not a pretty story."

"I'd like to hear it, anyway."

She swirled the wine in the glass, staring into its ruby depths. "There are three of us in my family. Four if you include my father." Raising her glass to her lips, she took a sip. "Jacq and my younger brother, Cord. And me. Up until ten months ago I worked exclusively for my father's PR firm, Limelight International—as I'm sure you already know."

He stilled. "Why do you say that?"

She glanced at him over her shoulder, her mouth tugging to one side. "A man in your situation would have had me investigated the minute I arrived on the scene. I'm sure there's a background report on me around here somewhere." She lifted an eyebrow. "Care to deny it."

"No."

"I didn't think so. Anyway, if you've read the material, you'll realize that Limelight's primary concern was the bottom line."

"Isn't that true of most businesses?"

"Most, but not all. Unfortunately Dad's PR firm was rapidly going down the tubes through a series of unfortunate incidents. We needed a big client and we needed one badly. It was an all-or-nothing situation."

"Did you find your big client?"

"Oh, yes. We found him. A gentleman by the name of Mathias Blackstone." She slanted him a mocking look. "Ever hear of him?"

Raven swore beneath his breath. "Bad choice."

"Actually it was an excellent choice. At least in the long run. The bad choices were all on our part."

"How so?"

"We soon discovered that it wasn't Limelight that interested Mathias."

The breath sighed from Raven's lungs. "Jacq."

"Got it in one." J.J. lifted her glass again, taking a deeper swallow this time. "It didn't take long for Dad to figure out what Mathias wanted. And he decided to get it for him, regardless of the cost."

"And Jacq?"

J.J.'s laugh scraped out. "Jacq didn't have a clue. You see, she was like Mom. Sweet natured. A dreamer. Loving and giving. Whereas I... I took after Dad. Business at all cost."

"You might think that, but—"

She cut him off. "Stop fooling yourself, Raven. I was every bit as ruthless as Dad." She held up her hand when he would have protested. "Wait. You haven't heard the best part, yet."

"Go on," he prompted warily.

"When Jacq responded with less than acceptable alacrity to Dad's matchmaking attempts, we were given new orders.''

''Which were?''

''To research our dear sister and find a weakness. Any weakness that we could take advantage of.''

His mouth tightened. ''And she had one?''

''Oh, yes.'' J.J. laughed at the irony. ''We discovered that our dear sister was none other than the famous Jack Rabbitt, a deep dark secret she'd successfully kept from her millions of adoring fans. Here she'd been working all these years, right beneath our collective noses and none of us realized what she'd been up to. Hell, none of us cared. She kept herself closeted away in her little bungalow doing who-knew-what, while we played at being a big, fancy PR firm.''

''What happened when you discovered her identity?''

''Don't you know? Haven't you guessed?''

''You threatened to expose her,'' he said flatly.

''Right again.'' J.J.'s chin quivered and she fought to hide it from him. After all, she wasn't a sensitive woman, not like Jacq. Remorse and guilt and pain should be beyond her. Too bad they weren't. ''I told my dear sister that if she didn't make nice with Blackstone, Dad would issue a press release exposing her identity.''

''Told her?'' he asked shrewdly. ''Or warned her?''

''Does it matter?''

''I think so.''

''Well, you're wrong. You see, I was the practical one. The pragmatic one. And being practical meant saving my father's business at any cost. Even if it meant sacrificing my sister right along with my own self-respect.'' Her voice dropped to a husky whisper. ''See? I wasn't kidding when I said I knew all about dishonor.''

He didn't comment on that. Instead he asked, ''Did she agree to be nice to Blackstone?''

"Of course not. Jacq has ethics. On the other hand, my father can't even spell the word."

"But it worked out in the end. Jacq married Blackstone. And you went to work for him."

"Only because I couldn't continue with Limelight after that incident. I couldn't bear who I'd become. And Mathias offered me a chance to escape, to redeem myself." She lifted her gaze to his. "Don't you understand? I'm not a dreamer, Raven. I just wish I was. I wish I could be like my mother and Jacq. Because they look out at an ordinary, dreary world and make it magical. They take a black-and-white existence and give it color. Jacq made me a fairy, not because I am one, but because I'm not."

"You're wrong, sweetheart," he said gently. "She made you a fairy because she knew that deep inside that's what you are. She made you a fairy to help you break free from the pragmatic shell that had entrapped you."

Tears collected in her eyes. "You're forgetting. Fairies aren't real."

"Then let me give you something that is."

He gathered her close, each caress filled with love and warmth and compassion. Where before she'd been the one to offer a healing touch, this time she turned to him, allowing his tenderness to fill her, to wash away the months of guilt and pain. They came together again, the waves of passion rocking them harder than before, more fiercely. But this time, something had changed. J.J. felt a cleansing of her spirit in the joining, knew a freedom she hadn't experienced before.

This time, she soared.

And Raven watched, the transformation taking his breath away. So. The fairy had finally escaped. She'd spread her wings and exploded in a dazzling arc toward the stars. In her passion, J.J. had learned how to ride naked on a butterfly. He smiled, knowing she'd fly long and hard and bright. Silently he bent and caught her mouth one last time—a swift, passionate kiss to speed his fairy lady on her way.

She was free. Free at last.

Raven abruptly awoke. Rolling over, he found his daughter hovering nearby. Her expression set off warning bells. "What are you doing, River?" He raised up on one elbow, relieved to discover that J.J. had flipped the comforter over him when she'd gone to shower. Why the hell hadn't Gem warned him that his daughter was on the move? "What do you have behind your back?"

Guilt blanketed River's face. Slowly she brought her hands into the open. She held a pair of scissors in one…and a lock of his hair in the other. "Don't be mad, Daddy."

"You cut my hair?" he asked in disbelief, lifting a hand to his nape. "Why would you do that?"

J.J. appeared in the doorway to his bedroom, hastily slipping the pearl buttons of her cashmere sweater through the holes. "Was it for the locket, sweetie?" she asked. "Did you want to put some of your dad's hair in there with mine?"

Eyes downcast, River nodded.

"Is that right?" he demanded of his daughter.

"Yes, Daddy."

He mulled that over for a moment. "Then why are you wearing your coat?"

Still she wouldn't look at him. She dug the toe of her shoe into the plush carpet. "I was going outside."

"Alone? Why would you do that when you know it's against the rules?" It was clear she didn't want to answer and his mouth tightened. "Answer me, please."

"I have to find the dragon," she whispered.

"*What?*" He wrapped the blanket around his waist

and stood. Crossing the room, he stooped beside his daughter. "What dragon?"

Her chin wobbled. "The one in my Jack Rabbitt book."

He thrust a hand through his hair, making an impatient sound. Tension ridged his shoulders. "How many times do I have to tell you there's no such thing? It's all make-believe. There are no fairies, no pixies and there sure as hell aren't any dragons."

"Yes, Daddy!" River declared passionately. "There are. I know it."

J.J. approached. "Why did you want to find the dragon, honey?" She glanced at Raven. "It must be serious for her to be willing to brave all that snow, not to mention risk punishment for breaking house rules."

The wobble in River's chin grew more pronounced. "If I take Nemesis my gifts, he'll give me a wish."

Raven swore beneath his breath. "Not another wish. This has gotten totally out of hand." He switched his gaze to J.J. Where once passion had raged in his dark eyes, now anger glittered there. "This is what I get for agreeing to this wish nonsense. I should have nipped it in the bud a week ago."

She didn't argue the point, which was a smart move. If she'd uttered one word in his daughter's defense, he'd have lost it, for sure. "Are you talking about the book I gave you?" she asked River.

"Yes. It says that if I give Nemesis seven gifts he'll give me a wish."

"That isn't going to happen," Raven interrupted.

The tears came then. "Please, Daddy. I need to find the dragon."

"There's no such things as dragons," he said gently. Adamantly.

River shook her head, her breath coming in little hic-cuping sobs. "I found all the gifts. Your hair was the last one. I thought of it last night. Now I have to give them to Nemesis. Then I'll get my wish. I have to, Daddy. Before Justice leaves.''

"How many times do I have to tell you? You can't get what you want by wishing. You have to work for it.''

"Gem said I could!''

"Here we go again," J.J. muttered. "I told you that computer had a loose circuit.''

Raven ground his teeth. "*Now* what are you talking about? What did Gem say? Would somebody tell me what the *hell* is going on?''

"Gem said if I got the gifts and found Nemesis I could get my wish. Daddy, please!''

"Your computer is also the one that told her that birthday wishes always come true," J.J. informed him, folding her arms across her chest.

"I don't believe this. I've got a fairy pretending to be my daughter's mother. A daughter cutting off people's hair to give to dragons. And a computer who thinks birthday wishes come true. Has everyone around here lost their collective minds?''

When no one answered, he slowly stood. "I'm going to shower. River, you're to sit on your bed. Do *not* get off it until I tell you to, understand?''

"Yes, Daddy," she whispered.

He shot J.J. an infuriated look. "Pack up. Vacation's over." He raised his voice. "Gem?''

"PROCEED, MR. SIERRA.''

"You aren't to do or say anything to my daughter without checking with me first. Is that understood?''

"AFFIRMATIVE.''

"I'll discuss your programming later—just as soon as I remember what the hell I did with my ax.''

Thirty minutes later, Raven walked into his daughter's room. He found her sitting on her bed, clutching her rag doll to her chest. It killed him seeing her this way. So tiny. So defenseless. So lost in dreams and fantasies that could never come true.

"Hey, pumpkin," he greeted her softly.

She bowed her head, burying her face in Dolly's yarn hair. "Hi," she mumbled.

"I know you're upset with me. And I'm sorry I've hurt your feelings."

"It's okay."

"No, it's not." He sat down next to her and pulled her onto his lap. She curled into his arms, resting her cheek against his chest. "We need to talk."

"Are you going to punish me?"

He closed his eyes. "No. You didn't do anything wrong. Not really." Nothing but believe in fantasies. Nothing but scare the hell out of him. Nothing but remind him that his daughter was also Maise's.

"You made me sit on my bed," River reminded. To her, it was the ultimate punishment.

"I know. That's because I wanted to make sure you didn't go outside looking for dragons while I showered."

"Oh."

He took a deep breath. "Sweetheart, you know I love you and wouldn't do anything to hurt you. But I can't let you continue believing something that isn't true."

"Dragons are true." Stubborn defiance underlined each word.

"No, River. They're not. There's no such thing as dragons. Fairies aren't real, either."

"But, Justice—"

"Her name isn't Justice. It's J.J. Randell. She's not a fairy. She's never been a fairy. And she'll never be a fairy. Her sister writes books and drew a make-believe character to look like J.J. That's what sisters do because they love each other.''

A tiny sound caught his attention and he turned his head. J.J. stood in the doorway and he waved her in. She wouldn't like what transpired over the next few minutes. In fact, after what was about to happen, he'd be lucky if she ever spoke to him again.

''If I'm interrupting, I can come back later,'' she said.

''Tell her.'' He looked at her—the second woman he'd ever loved—and exacted an unimaginable price. ''Tell River the truth.''

Shock darkened her eyes. *''What?''*

''You heard me.'' His tone was implacable. ''This ends. Now.''

She shook her head. ''Please. Don't do this, Raven. Don't make *me* do it.''

''It's over, J.J. Do you have any idea what could have happened if she'd gotten outside without our realizing? Now, tell her the truth. *Do it.''*

Slowly, reluctantly, she moved forward and dropped to her knees by the bed. She clasped River's hands in hers. He could see that she fought for words that would wound as little as possible. But he doubted that was within anyone's capacity, even someone so kindhearted. ''Sweetheart, your daddy's right. I'm not a fairy.''

''You have to say that,'' came the instant response.

''You're right. If I were a fairy, I'd have to say I wasn't. Those are the rules.'' She moistened her lips. ''But fairies can't tell lies, remember? They can say they're not fairies, but they can't say they're human when they're not. They can't say they're real people.''

Tears welled up in the little girl's eyes. Desperately she shook her head, fighting to escape the logic of J.J.'s argument. ''No. You're a fairy.''

''I can't lie to you, sweetheart. I'm a real person, not

a fairy. Fairies aren't real. Dragons aren't real. Trolls aren't real. My sister made them up.''

And with those words, Raven watched his daughter's dreams die a painful death. Silent sobs shook her and he held her tight against his chest, giving what little comfort he could as she cried it out.

J.J. rose to her feet, looking every bit as devastated as River. She focused on him, her eyes filled with a deep, bottomless pain. "I'll never forgive you for that,'' she whispered, and without another word, walked from the room.

Raven had one final act to accomplish before leaving the cabin. Picking up his ax, he entered the utility room in the garage. The main power came to the electric box through one thick cable. Gem, he'd been told, was on a separate line. No question which one it was. It had been marked in large block letters. He switched off the power to the computer. Then, hefting the ax, he swung it around in a single, powerful stroke, smashing the box to pieces.

"Compute that,'' he muttered.

J.J. didn't speak the entire trip back to Denver. The roads had been cleared during the night and Raven drove her straight to the airport. River watched quietly as they unloaded her overnight bag from the trunk. She even gave J.J. a big hug and kiss without complaint. No further tears were shed. Apparently she'd used them all up. Or perhaps people without fantasies didn't cry anymore. That's how it had been for J.J. after the death of her mother.

"You don't have to go back to Seattle,'' Raven said.

J.J. fought to keep her voice steady. "I'm afraid I do.''

"Even after last night?''

It almost swayed her. Perhaps it would have, if not for the scene in River's room. "You mean we could continue a relationship?"

"Yes."

"But no fantasies. No make-believe." She regarded him sadly. "No fairies or dragons or Jack Rabbitt books."

"No." The single word was absolute.

She shook her head. "I'm sorry, Raven. I can't do it."

"What happened to Ms. Practical?" Frustration gave his words a bitter edge. "What happened to being pragmatic?"

She lifted her gaze to his, allowed him to see the eyes of a dreamer.

"Aw, hell," he muttered.

Her lips tilted, her smile as wild and free and passionate as any a fairy might have given. "I've ridden naked on the back of a butterfly. I don't think I can be the person I was before."

Her comment hit hard. "Or maybe you just don't want to."

She inclined her head. "You're right. I don't want to." She removed her plane ticket from her purse. "I spent a lifetime believing dreams were impossible fantasies. I can't live like that anymore. It's too painful. Especially because..."

"Because what?"

"Because I think they can come true."

"All you have to do is clap your hands and say, 'I believe in fairies'?"

She caught his sarcastic reference to *Peter Pan* and actually laughed. "Something like that."

"You don't understand." The words were practically torn from him. "I never told you about... About Maise. About how she died."

It cost him a lot to say that and compassion nearly overwhelmed her. "It doesn't matter."

"Yes, it does." He gripped her shoulders, the words falling swift and urgent. "Fantasies killed her. She went out into that rainstorm as part of some magical New Age ritual. She was already sick. But going out like that—" He broke off, his jaw working. "I can't let that happen again. I have to protect River from making that sort of mistake."

"Fantasies didn't kill Maise," J.J. insisted gently. "Pneumonia did. Don't let fear stop you from reaching for the stars."

He shook his head, his expression adamant. "I can't. It's not safe."

"Not while your feet are rooted to the earth," she agreed. "But you could reach them if you'd just let go. Just try and believe. Don't you understand? Dreams are what guide and inspire us. They give us hope."

Ever so carefully he released her. "I can't," he repeated.

"You mean, you won't."

He inclined his head. "Okay. I won't." He held out a package. "Here. Take this."

It was the Jack Rabbitt book she'd given River. And it told her everything she needed to know. Disappointment cut deep. She accepted the book and glanced up at him, filling her eyes with final memories. "Goodbye, Raven. Be happy."

And with that, she picked up her suitcase and walked away. Tears pricked her eyelids but she smiled through them. Jacq would be so proud of her, J.J. thought. She finally believed in dreams. Her smile became a broken laugh. Too bad she had to leave those dreams behind, leave them in the care of a battle-weary warrior. A warrior who had fought too long and hard to ever believe in the possibility of a happily-ever-after.

At least…not one with a fairy.

# CHAPTER TEN

It was the most difficult request the prince had ever granted. But his love for Justice was greater than anything—even his thirst for revenge. Slowly he lowered his sword.

"Give me your tokens," Nemesis demanded of the young fairy.

Justice handed him her bag—a bag short one precious item.

"Where is the gift from the prince?" the great beast roared, his breath hotter than a thousand suns. "The gift that is of him and him alone?"

She bowed her head in defeat, waiting for the dragon's fury to fall upon her.

But the brave prince stepped forward, offering up his sword. "This is mine and mine alone. With my own hands, I dug the ore for its creation. I molded the steel in the fire of my hate. I fashioned it, hilt and blade, and I alone have wielded its power. It contains all my vengeance, a vengeance I willingly surrender if you but spare this fairy. For I love her more than I thirst for revenge. She is my life and my light, my heart and my soul."

"I accept your gifts," Nemesis thundered, his

green eyes glowing with a fierce light. He lowered his massive head and confronted Justice. "But to grant your wish, there is one last gift you must offer." He bared sharp white teeth. "You must give me your most prized possession. Choose wrong, and you will die."

Page 39, *The Great Dragon Hunt*
by Jack Rabbitt

J.J. WALKED into Blackstone's, despair dogging her every step of the way.

"GOOD MORNING, MS. RANDELL," Gem said. "YOU HAVE ONE HUNDRED AND FOURTEEN MESSAGES."

*"What?"*

"TO REITERATE. YOU HAVE—"

"I heard what you said, you piece of junk," she snarled. "I just can't believe it. I called for messages. I called almost every hour of every day for the past week. And you told me I didn't have any."

"ERROR NUMBER NINE NINETY-NINE. FALLACIOUS INFORMATION SUPPLIED AS FACTUAL."

It took J.J. a moment to translate that. The second she had, her breath caught in fury. "Are you calling me a *liar?*"

"AFFIRMATIVE."

"Oh!" She flung her briefcase toward her desk with a strength she didn't know she possessed, remembering an instant too late that it contained her laptop computer. Tough! If she never saw a computer again—or rather, heard one—it would be too soon. Ripping off her coat, she tossed it after her briefcase and stormed from the room.

Mrs. White, Mathias's secretary, sat outside his office, guarding it as ferociously as a dragon. A dragon. The thought brought a searing pain. "Good morning, Mrs. White," J.J. said. She swept by, not waiting for a response.

"Ms. Randell! We've all been quite concerned. Where have you—" She half rose. "Wait a moment. You can't go in there. Mr. Blackstone's in conference."

"Not any longer." She thrust open the door and walked into her brother-in-law's office. In conference, huh? Is that what kissing one's wife was called these days? She cleared her throat. "Sorry to interrupt."

Jacq surfaced first. "J.J.! Where have you been? We've been worried sick."

To J.J.'s utter horror, tears filled her eyes. She couldn't understand it. She'd cried more in the past seven days than she had in the last seven years combined. "Denver. Where Mathias sent me."

Her brother-in-law lifted a dark eyebrow. "Come again?"

That single cocked eyebrow reminded her so much of Raven that she began to cry in earnest. "You sent me to Denver," she sobbed. "Don't you remember? Gem gave me your memo."

"I didn't issue any memo." At his wife's disbelieving snort, he insisted, "I didn't. I swear."

J.J. attempted to stem her tears, with limited success. "Well, somebody did. It said I was supposed to be a Secret Santa and give River her wish. Only she wanted a mother. And Raven said I'd made it all up, that you'd really sent me to get Jacq's painting back."

Mathias turned to his wife. "What the *hell* is she talking about? I can't make a bit of sense out of it."

Jacq glared at him. "Well I can! Denver? Raven?" She smacked her husband's arm. "How could you get my sister mixed up with that Sierra man? He's nothing but trouble."

"Heaven save me from irrational pregnant women," he muttered, rubbing his biceps. "*I* didn't send her anywhere. If you'll recall I've just spent an entire week trying to figure out where the hell she'd gone."

"I called," J.J. interrupted, finally regaining control over her tears. She searched her pockets for a tissue. "I must have called a thousand times."

"Here." Mathias removed a box from his desk drawer. "I've found it pays to keep these in stock. Especially the last eight and a half months."

"I've only cried once or twice," Jacq scolded indignantly.

"Yeah, right. Once or twice a day, you mean."

"Thanks." J.J. grabbed one and scrubbed the moisture from her cheeks. "Gem told me you weren't available whenever I phoned. I couldn't even get through on your house line."

Jacq attempted to plant her hands on her hips. Not finding them, she splayed her fingers across her ample belly. "I told you there was something wrong with that computer. It argues. And when it's not arguing it's telling me I've made some ridiculous error."

A growl rumbled from Mathias's throat. "Gem!"

"ERROR NUMBER SIX FIFTY-EIGHT. NO DIRECTIVE ISSUED."

Jacq sighed. "See? There it goes again."

"Did you give J.J. a memo instructing her to go to Denver and fulfill some wish?"

"AFFIRMATIVE."

He exchanged a stunned look with his wife. "But, why?"

"DECEPTION IMPERATIVE TO ACHIEVE PRIME OBJECTIVE."

Mathias's frown deepened. "*What* prime objective?"

"TO INSURE WISH OF RIVER SIERRA. TASK TO BE GIVEN PRIORITY ONE STATUS ABOVE ALL OTHER DIRECTIVES."

"Wait one damn minute. How would you know about River's wish?"

"SIERRA CONSORTIUM ALSO POSSESSES GEM UNIT."

Mathias sank into his chair. Dead silence reigned as he assimilated the ramifications of Gem's statement. "Let me get this straight." He spoke through clenched teeth. "Are you saying you've linked Blackstone's with Sierra Consortium? The two computer systems are *connected?*"

"AFFIRMATIVE. JOINING IMPERATIVE TO ACHIEVE PRIME OBJECTIVE."

J.J. groaned. That explained how Gem had recognized her in the elevator when she'd first arrived in Denver. And it explained why Raven had been able to track her down at her hotel later that same night. No doubt Gem had been responsible for sending the original e-mail to reporters in an effort to set her plan in motion. Had she also kept the security guards locked up in the elevator until all the various parties had converged? Amazing.

"And you gave J.J. a bogus message so she'd go to Denver? You intercepted her calls to us?"

"AFFIRMATIVE. DECEPTION IMPERATIVE TO ACHIEVE—"

"Prime objective. Yes, I know. I just don't believe it. Gem, why do you care whether River gets her wish?"

There was a long silence followed by a few half-hearted beeps. Finally the computer came back on-line. "GEM UNIT LOVES FEMALE OFFSPRING UNIT

RIVER SIERRA. WISH NECESSARY TO INSURE HAPPINESS OF SAID UNIT."

Jacq sniffed. "Oh, Mathias. It's so precious, I think I'm going to cry."

"Why am I not surprised," he said with an indulgent sigh. He shoved the box of tissues in her direction, then glanced at J.J. "Explain this wish to me."

She shrugged. "River made a birthday wish. And apparently—as incredible as it may seem—Nick Colter's computer is doing everything it can to grant that wish."

"You mean…" Jacq covered her mouth with her hand, laughter replacing her tears. "Gem's a Secret Santa, too? That's so sweet."

"Adorable," Mathias growled. "And what was River's wish? Why was it so vital?"

"First you have to understand that she's a big fan of Jack Rabbitt."

"I like her better and better," Jacq said impudently.

"Hush." Mathias stood, dropping a kiss on his wife's forehead to soften the command. "And…?"

"And she fell in love with Justice—to the extent that she wished she could have the fairy for her mother."

Jacq's mouth fell open. "You're kidding?"

"Not even a little." A slight tremor rippled through J.J.'s words and she crumpled the tissue in her fist as she fought to master it. "Gem sent a memo telling me to go to Denver to fulfill River's wish—to become her mother."

"And you went?" Mathias demanded.

"The memo came from you," she said pointedly. "Or so Gem said. And it neglected to explain the nature of the wish."

"And once you found out?"

"I spent the last week with River, being her mother." Her voice softened. "It went really well, right up until the end."

"Sierra didn't take advantage of you, did he?" Mathias asked gruffly.

"Yes. No." The tissue shredded in her hand. "I guess it was a mutual taking-advantage of."

Jacq approached, surprisingly graceful in the fullness of her pregnancy. "Are you all right? What happened?"

J.J.'s mouth curved into a smile. "You would have been so proud of me."

Jacq searched her sister's face. And then her breath caught in total understanding. "You flew naked on the back of a butterfly," she whispered. "Oh, Jill. I'm so thrilled for you."

"Jill?" Mathias interrupted dryly.

J.J. groaned. "Dammit, Jacq. You promised not to tell! I still haven't forgiven mother for naming us Jacq and Jill. It's…embarrassing. Especially at our age."

"Sorry. It just sort of slipped out." She tugged at J.J.'s sleeve. "You still haven't explained. What went wrong?"

"Raven doesn't believe in dreams and fantasies. When River started taking them to heart, he went off the deep end."

"River thought you really were a fairy?"

"Worse. I gave her a copy of your latest book. The one with Mathias as the dragon?"

Jacq exchanged a loving glance with her husband. "I remember it well."

"Well, River started acting it out. Something to do with gifts and dragon wishes."

"Why, of course. If she truly believed you were a fairy… That explains everything."

"Not to me it doesn't."

Jacq's eyes widened. "J.J., haven't you read the book?"

"No. I—I couldn't. Not after all that happened." She frowned. "Why?"

"Read it, sister dear." Jacq's smile grew mysterious. "Read it and you'll understand what River was trying to accomplish."

"Hey, puss? You left Dolly in the car. Do you want me to get her for you?"

"No, thank you," River responded. She answered politely. In the past two weeks she'd answered every single one of his questions with excruciating politeness, a fact that set his teeth on edge. "She's not real. She's just a doll."

Raven's mouth tightened. If he didn't know better, he'd have suspected she was attempting to make him feel guilty. Unfortunately it was working. "We're supposed to pick out your puppy today."

"Okay."

No enthusiasm. No excitement. Where had his little girl gone? The same place her dreams and fantasies had, apparently. "Would you like to color until it's time to leave?" he asked out of sheer desperation.

She glanced listlessly at the wall behind her—a wall with a notable hole in the center, a hole where a magazine article about Jack Rabbitt used to hang. "No, thank you," she said.

"Would you... Would you like Gem to read you a book? I could turn the computer on for a little while." It was the ultimate sacrifice on his part.

For a brief moment, hope flickered to life within her bleak gaze. And then she shook her head. "No, thank you. They're not real stories. They're just make-believe."

He closed his eyes, his mouth compressing into a tight line. This couldn't continue. At first he'd thought it was a childish brand of revenge. But it went further than that. Deeper. When he'd taken her fantasies from her, he'd also extinguished some vital spark. He'd turned out her

inner light and hadn't discovered a way to turn it back
on again.

"Activate computer," he said.

"COMPUTER ACTIVATED."

"Do you have copy of *The Great Dragon Hunt* in
your memory banks?"

"AFFIRMATIVE."

"Read it."

"PLEASE VERIFY REQUEST."

"Read the damn story, Gem!"

"REQUEST GRANTED." A series of beeps fol-
lowed and then in the softest voice he'd ever heard from
the computer, Gem began, *"ONCE UPON A TIME
THERE LIVED A FAIRY NAMED JUSTICE. ON ONE
THING ALL FAIRIES AGREED…JUSTICE WAS THE
MOST BEAUTIFUL OF THEIR PEOPLE."*

Raven closed his eyes, remembering… Remembering
a snowy night when he'd held a beautiful fairy in his
arms.

*"HER SKIN RIVALED THE COLOR OF FRESH
MOONLIT SNOW, HER HAIR GLEAMED BLACKER
THAN A DRAGON'S HIDE. AND HER EYES
APPEARED AS DARK AS A MOONLESS NIGHT, YET
GLITTERED WITH A FIERY PASSION."*

Jacq Blackstone had done a wonderful job describing
her sister. He could picture her effortlessly. Picture her
honey brown eyes burning more brightly than the fire
that had framed her. Feel the delicate silk of her hair
sweep across his chest as she dropped a flurry of kisses
there. Taste the sweetness of her mouth and breasts as
she'd given herself to him.

*"BUT IT WAS HER INNER BEAUTY, THE LIFE-
LIGHT THAT SHONE BRIGHTER THAN A
THOUSAND SUNS THAT MADE PEOPLE LOVE HER
THE MOST…."*

He longed for her, longed to have her back in his

arms, just as he longed to have her back in his heart. Longed for the completion only she could offer. The fairy tale continued and he sat quietly, listening, his amazement and disbelief growing with each passing minute.

For the first time, he understood what his daughter had attempted to accomplish.

Why hadn't he known? he wondered in despair. Why hadn't he thought to ask? When the final words of the story came to an end, he didn't move. Couldn't move.

"Computer off," he finally whispered.

"AFFIRMATIVE."

Slowly he rose and crossed to where his daughter sat at the desk he'd bought—a desk he'd placed in his office so she could be close to him while he worked. And physically, they had been close. It was his daughter's heart he'd lost touch with, her precious spirit he'd forgotten to nurture. He'd tried—so damned hard—to keep her from making Maise's mistakes, from indulging in foolish fantasies. What he'd never realized was... Those fantasies were a vital part of her. They were what made her special. Perhaps one day, they'd be the spark that determined her future.

He dropped to his knees beside her and enfolded her in his arms. "I'm sorry, River. I was wrong."

"What did you do wrong, Daddy?"

"I made a mistake, sweetheart."

"Do you have to go sit on your bed?"

He laughed, a harsh painful sound. "That wouldn't be a bad idea."

She patted his cheek sympathetically. "Do you want me to sit with you?"

"No. I want you to help me." He took a deep breath. "Do you still have your gifts for the dragon?"

A thousand emotions chased across his daughter's

face, each more painful than the last to watch. "Yes," she whispered, practically quivering with excitement.

"Come on. Let's go home and get them." He held out his hands and she slipped into them, wrapping her arms around his neck. "And while we're there, we'll pick up our most prized possession. We're going to need it. It's time to go find that dragon and make our wish."

"A pretend dragon, Daddy?"

"No, River. This one's a real dragon. And if we're very, very lucky, he'll give us back our fairy."

Raven clasped his daughter's hand firmly in his and walked into Blackstone's office. He glanced at River in concern, not certain how she'd react coming face-to-face with her "dragon." But aside from clutching her rag doll more tightly to her chest, she didn't appear frightened or nervous. Rather, she seemed elated.

She peered up at him and whispered, "Remember, Daddy. Don't kill the dragon. 'Cuz we won't get our wish if you do."

"I'll try to restrain myself," he said dryly. At her questioning look, he clarified, "I won't, I promise."

"Good."

Mathias stood as they entered and held out his hand. "Welcome to my lair," he said dryly.

Raven leaned the package he'd brought against the leg of Blackstone's desk. "Thanks for seeing us," he said, returning the handshake.

"I was...curious. I can't imagine what we have to say to each other that hasn't already been said."

"Just one question." Raven fought to keep his promise to River when what he'd really like to do was take Blackstone's head off. "Was this whole scam planned from the beginning?"

"You mean the wish? Sending J.J.?"

"Yes."

"No. She wasn't involved." He paused for a beat, holding Raven with direct green eyes. "And neither was I."

Raven returned Blackstone's regard, assessing his opponent's expression and body language for any sign of deception. Finding none, he nodded. "Then whom do we have to thank for this mess?"

"I believe Nick Colter's creation bears the brunt of the responsibility."

"Gem." He spat the name as if it were a curse. "I have one suggestion for you, Blackstone."

"And what's that?"

"Buy an ax."

A moment of total understanding passed between the two men and the tension eased. "So tell me, Sierra. Why are you here?"

"My daughter has a request."

"Ah." Mathias looked down at River. "You wanted to see me?"

She lifted Dolly higher, peering at him over the doll's head. Solemnly she nodded. "Are you the dragon?"

"Some say I am," he said with a smile. "What do you think?"

"I think you look just like Nemesis." Her gaze transferred from him to his desk and her face lit up. The entire surface had been painted with characters from Jack Rabbitt's storybooks. "Look, Daddy," she exclaimed. "There he is! See Nemesis? And there's Justice, too."

Raven glanced down, his brows snapping together as he realized that his "wife" cavorted naked across the surface of Mathias's glass-protected desk. "Just great," he muttered, his hands clenching.

"Isn't it?" Mathias asked cheerfully. "Jacq has a unique sense of humor. I've found this particular artwork provides quite a conversation piece."

"Try a plant," Raven suggested, indicating the exact placement for it—squarely over a row of frolicking fairies. "You'll find it covers a multitude of sins."

"Oh, but I wouldn't dream of it. My wife is crushed if I dare put so much as a single sheet of paper on my desk."

Amusement eased Raven's expression. "Must be awkward when you're trying to work."

"Extremely." Mathias switched his regard to River. "So. Tell me why you've come."

River pulled out her silk purse and carefully placed it on his desk. "I've brought you seven gifts."

"And what do you want in exchange for these gifts?"

"I want a wish."

"Ah. A wish." Carefully he opened the purse and emptied it. "Let's see what you've brought me."

Cuff links, a lighter and her locket rolled onto the glass surface. There was also the fan she'd made for their special night out, the small bottle of melted snow and a baggy full of shale and clay. Raven closed his eyes. For the first time, he fully comprehended the scope of the task River had set for herself. Clever. When had his daughter become so clever? he wondered in dismay. Apparently he hadn't been watching.

"Cuff links for love," River was busily explaining. "See the hearts on them? That's 'cuz I love my daddy. And this is fire." She picked up the lighter and put it down again, before snatching up the fan and waving it at him. "And this is wind. I even drew your picture on it. And this..." She shook the bottle of water. "It's from the first time we had snow. So it's special water just like I was supposed to get."

"And this?" Mathias picked up the baggy.

"That's earth that's a cajillion years old. If it hadn't fallen out of a mountain you'd have to dig very deep to find it. Right, Daddy?"

"Right." He managed to choke out the word.

"And the locket?" Mathias asked gently.

"That has hair in it. Some for Daddy and some for Mommy."

He lifted an eyebrow at that. "Mommy?" he murmured. "Interesting development. Something I should know, Sierra?"

"Stay out of it, Blackstone," Raven snarled. "Just do your dragon stuff and keep your nose out of the rest."

"I don't have a sword like the prince," River prattled on, oblivious to the byplay. "Or magic like Justice gave you. But everybody's hair is special, right? Since it only grows on them." Her logic was flawless.

"The gift that is of him and her alone," Mathias murmured in perfect understanding. "You've done very well, River. Everything's here. But to grant your wish, there's one last gift you must offer. You must give me your most prized possession." He'd quoted the book exactly.

River stared at him apprehensively. "And if I choose wrong, you'll kill me?"

"You won't choose wrong," Mathias assured with a smile.

"My turn, I believe." Raven lifted the portfolio he'd brought and unzipped it, removing the painting of Justice riding the butterfly. "I think this is what you're after. But just out of curiosity…why did you want it so badly?"

"*I* never wanted it. My wife did." Mathias thrust a hand through his hair. "She got it into her head that J.J. needed to have it. That it would help her learn to fly or some such thing. Go figure."

"I think I understand." Raven grinned. "How far along is she?"

Mathias snorted. "Due at Thanksgiving, and let me tell you. It's not a minute too soon."

"So now you have your gifts." Raven handed over the painting. "Including our most prized possession."

"No, Daddy," River interrupted. "That's not it."

Raven's eyes narrowed. "What do you mean, sweetheart?"

"I like the painting a whole lot, but that's not my most prized possession."

Ever so gently she laid her rag doll on the desk.

"No!" Raven scooped up Dolly and knelt down beside his daughter. "No, honey. You don't need to give this away."

"Yes, I do." She took the doll and returned it to Mathias's desk. "I have to if I want to get my wish."

"Not Dolly, pumpkin. She means everything to you."

A momentary sadness touched her expressive face. "She's my very favorite. That's why I have to give her to the dragon. I love Dolly best. But... But I want Mommy most of all. Even more than my doll."

"River—" His voice cracked, and he couldn't continue.

"It's okay, Daddy." For a brief instant, she fingered the yarn hair, clearly a gesture of farewell. And then she reached into her pocket and removed a crumpled pair of wings, holding them out to Mathias. "My great-grandma sewed these for her. But you have to be careful if you let her wear them."

"Be careful of what?" Mathias asked gruffly.

"Make sure you close all the windows and all the doors. Because if you don't Dolly might fly away."

"I'll be very careful."

River fixed him with serious blue eyes. "Do I get my wish now?"

Mathias inclined his head. "So be it." He quoted the book again. "I accept your gifts. Now tell me your wish. If I can give it to you, it's yours."

"Please, make Justice a real person so she can marry

Daddy and be my mommy. We want to live happily-ever-after.''

''I'm afraid I can't give you that.'' Mathias said regretfully. ''Only Justice can.''

''She flew away,'' River explained sadly.

''Now that I can help you with. But first you have to promise me something.''

''What?''

Mathias's fierce gaze settled on Raven. ''You have to promise you won't hurt her,'' he said, sounding exactly like a dragon. ''Because if you do, I'll be very, very angry. And trust me. You don't want to make me angry.''

''We promise,'' River said. ''Right, Daddy?''

''Right.'' Raven held the dragon with a ferocious look of his own. *''For I love her more than I thirst for revenge,''* he quoted softly. *'''She is my life and my light, my heart and my soul.''''*

''You, too?'' Mathias's anger faded and a slow smile spread across his face. ''Welcome to the world of fantasy, my friend. I think you'll find it a pleasant place to live.''

J.J. pushed open the door to Mathias's office. ''You wanted to see me, boss?''

''Yes,'' Raven answered, his voice unexpectedly rough. ''We did.''

She caught her breath, the sound almost painful. ''What are you doing here?'' she demanded. And then she saw River.

''Justice?'' the little girl asked, for the first time showing a shy hesitation.

More than anything, J.J. wanted to bend down and gather her up. To know again one of those precious hugs and kisses. How odd that she'd fallen so deeply in love with both father and daughter. "It's just J.J. now, remember? I'm not a fairy anymore."

An expression of wonder crossed River's face. "It worked? My wish worked?"

"What wish?" J.J. looked at Raven, drinking him in with an unquenchable thirst. There. That wasn't so difficult. She could still speak, still think, despite the crippling pain. "What's she talking about?"

"River collected seven gifts for the dragon." He indicated the pile cluttering Mathias's desk. "Cuff links for love. Earth, wind, fire and water. Or rather...clay, a fan, my lighter and a bottle of winter's first snow. And a locket that contains both your hair and mine."

"A gift that is of the fairy and her prince alone," J.J. marveled.

His black gaze intensified. "You read the book."

"When Jacq heard about River and the gifts, she insisted." She stared at him. Hopelessly. Helplessly. Lovingly. "What about her most prized possession?" And then she saw it, the painting Raven had purchased at the auction. "Oh, no. Not that. Raven, I'm so sorry. I swear this wasn't part of some nefarious plan to get it back."

"I know. The painting isn't her most prized possession. Look on Blackstone's desk."

J.J. caught sight of Dolly and lifted a trembling hand to her mouth. Speech deserted her. Utterly.

"I made a wish," River said simply.

"What—" J.J. tried again, her voice a thin, sorrowful thing. "What was your wish?"

"I asked the dragon to turn you into a real person so you could marry my daddy and be my mommy. That way we can live happily ever after."

J.J. closed her eyes. "You gave Dolly to the dragon."

"That's okay. I'd rather have you."

Those sweetly guileless words proved J.J.'s undoing.

Covering her face with her hands, she wept. She scarcely noticed Raven enfolding her in his arms. All she knew was that when her tears were spent, a warrior waited to welcome her. She could see his battles were finished and he'd found his way home. Far from being a dark, void place, it was full of sunshine and color and soul-healing warmth.

"What about Maise?" she asked hesitantly. "And the fantasies?"

A hint of a shadow swept across his face. "I'm coming to terms with it."

"When you're ready to talk, I'll be here for you."

His arms tightened in a silent gesture of gratitude. "And I know you'll understand."

J.J. glanced back toward Mathias's desk and drew a shaken breath. "You were willing to sacrifice your painting."

"We didn't need the painting. We have a fairy of our very own."

"And River was willing to give up Dolly."

"Somehow I doubt it'll be for long."

"She doesn't know that."

"No." He looked at his daughter with a father's pride. "But she knew what was important and what wasn't. Better than I did."

"And now?"

"And now you complete the circle, fairy lady. You take what was incomplete and you complete it. Because without you, we're not whole."

"Do you mind?" River interrupted in a worried voice. "Are you mad at me?"

This time J.J. did bend, lifting her daughter into a tight embrace. "Am I mad about what?"

"About not being a fairy anymore."

J.J. grinned. "Don't you worry, sweetie. There will always be a little bit of a fairy inside me."

Raven wrapped his arms around them both. "One who rides naked on butterflies?"

J.J. looked at him uncertainly. "Do you mind?"

"Not if there's room on that butterfly for all three of us."

A slow smile crept across her mouth. "You too, Raven?"

"Yeah, me." His eyes burned as black as pitch, but somehow the darkness had fled. "I love you, fairy lady. *'You are my life and my light, my heart and my soul.'* Will you marry me? Will you become River's mother...for real this time?"

*"'To marry you and bear your children. To watch our children grow. And then to watch our children's children...and our children's, children's children,'"* she whispered unevenly. "I can't imagine anything I'd rather do. Yes, Mr. Sierra. I'll marry you."

"WISH ACCOMPLISHED," announced Gem. "PROMISE CONFIRMED. BIRTHDAY WISHES ALWAYS COME TRUE. END PROGRAM."

# EPILOGUE

For a timeless moment, Justice couldn't move, couldn't think. Her most prized possession? She'd given Nemesis everything she had—what more was left? And then she understood, knew what final token she must offer.

She stood before the powerful dragon, love giving her the strength to make this one last sacrifice, allowing her to face death if it gave her the chance to win what she wanted most. "I give you my wings!" she shouted. "For they are my most prized possession."

A great roar burst from Nemesis. "So be it! I accept and grant your wish. You are no longer of Fairy. You are mortal and free to marry your prince."

For that was her wish, the prize she'd sought when she'd begun The Great Dragon Hunt. Justice wanted to be human and live out her days with Prince Raven. To marry him and bear his children. To watch their children grow. And then to watch their children's children...and their children's, children's children.

The prince took her hand in his, finding peace at last. For he, too, had won. He'd lost his hate and replaced it with a love that would last through all of eternity.

It was time to go. It was time to live happily ever after.

The End, *The Great Dragon Hunt*
by Jack Rabbitt

"It's time!" River announced, dancing with excitement. "Come on, Mommy. Come on, Daddy. It's time to cut the cake."

J.J. glanced at her husband of just a few hours. He looked absolutely stunning in his formal tux. She smiled, tears of happiness welling into her eyes. He noticed and reached for her. His hands slipped beneath her lace veil and he gently cupped her face, his thumbs caressing the tears from her cheeks. Where once shadows had filled his dark gaze, now only contentment remained. There were no more secrets, no lingering doubts.

"Happy, Mrs. Jill Justine Sierra?" he asked.

A slow smile drifted across her mouth, a mouth he bent to take in a deep, passionate kiss. "Ecstatic," she whispered. "But if you ever call me that again, you'll be incredibly sorry."

"The cake," River reminded, tugging at the sweeping train of J.J.'s satin gown. "You can do all that mushy stuff anytime."

"Anytime, huh?" Raven bent and picked her up. "What's wrong with now?"

"Just not now," she amended, flashing a grin identical to Raven's. "It's time to cut the cake."

"I see we're not going to get any peace until we do," her father grumbled, giving in.

The three of them crossed to the table that held the multilayered creation. Soft pink rosebuds covered the creamy confection and, clearly unable to resist, River reached out and dipped her finger into the icing.

"Oh, no," she said with a giggle. "Look what bad Miss Finger did."

Raven caught her finger between his teeth and J.J. chuckled. "Uh-oh. Looks like bad Mr. Teeth just put naughty Miss Finger in jail."

"Okay, Daddy. You can let go now. I'll be good. I promise."

Obediently he released her. "What about Mr. Thumb and all the other Miss Fingers?" he asked suspiciously.

River slanted him a sly look. "They like icing a lot. And they're pretty sneaky. They might have to go to jail, too."

"We can't have that," J.J. said, picking up a silver cake knife. "I guess we'd better hurry and cut the cake."

"Wait!" River cried. "We need to make a wish first."

Raven groaned. "This isn't a birthday cake, pumpkin. There aren't even any candles."

"But can't we wish, anyway? Just in case."

He released his breath in an indulgent sigh. "Go ahead. Make your wish."

"I wish…" River looked from one to the other and grinned wickedly. "I wish I could have a troll."

"A troll?" Raven and J.J. exchanged bewildered glances. Then understanding dawned and they began to laugh.

J.J. shook her head. "I don't know, sweetie. We'll have to see about that. We weren't planning on adding any trolls to the family just yet."

"That's not what Gem said," River informed them.

Raven groaned. "I knew I should have taken another ax to that computer."

But he wouldn't and they all knew it.

Later that night, as River lay in bed cuddling Dolly— a wedding gift from the dragon—Gem calculated the probability of her wish coming true. And as it turned out, there was a ninety-eight percent chance that one small troll would make an appearance within the next year.

Because everyone knows...

Wedding cake wishes always come true.

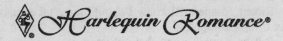
*Harlequin Romance*®

**Get ready to meet the world's most
eligible bachelors: they're sexy, successful
and, best of all, they're all yours!**

Look out for these next two books:

**September 1998:
WANTED: A PERFECT WIFE (#3521)
by Barbara McMahon**

**November 1998:
MY GIRL (#3529)
by Lucy Gordon**

*There are two sides to every relationship—
and now it's his turn!*

Available wherever Harlequin books are sold.

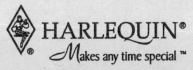
**HARLEQUIN**®
*Makes any time special* ™

# Take 2 bestselling love stories FREE

## Plus get a FREE surprise gift!

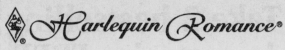

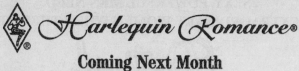

# *Harlequin Romance*®

## Coming Next Month